TAMING HER MATE

The Nightstar Shifters 6

ARIEL MARIE

"There is never a time or place for true love. It happens accidentally, in a heartbeat, in a single flashing, throbbing moment."

Sarah Dessen

CHAPTER ONE

"There. I'm finally unpacked." Kardia Markway sighed. Her small cabin was perfect for her. The sense of home overcame her. She wasn't sure if it was the house or the town. But all she knew, she felt safe and secure in Howling Valley.

It had been two weeks since she had arrived. Her grandfather had made arrangements for her to move to the little Southern California town.

Why had she needed to move to Howling Valley?

Mainly due to her last name.

She was a Markway, and her family was one of

the oldest shifter families around. Her grandfather was a member of the council, and due to recent events where the council had stripped an alpha of his pack and power, there was heat on their family's name.

Kardia glanced at the clock on the wall. She was expecting company, and knowing her grandfather, he would be on time.

"I better hurry up," she mumbled. She ran into her bedroom and snagged her sandals. She threw them on and went into the bathroom to take one last look at herself. Her golden-brown skin glowed, her amber eyes were wide and almond shaped. She considered herself pretty with her dark hair resting on her shoulders. She had recently washed it and decided to flat iron it.

Kardia grabbed her comb and ran it though her hair again to ensure she was presentable for the meeting she was about to attend with her grandfather. Satisfied with her appearance, she left the bathroom and went back into the living room. The cabin was a cute two-bedroom home with ample room for her. It was in the middle of the woods located on the Nightstar Pack grounds. She had yet to meet her neighbors who were not too far from her cabin.

A knock sounded at the door.

"On time as usual," she muttered.

Opening the door, she was met by a council guard while the others stood next to the SUVs parked in front of her home. One nearest the first truck opened the back door, and her grandfather stepped out. He was dressed in his signature robes that were black and adorned with gold decorations. His dark dreadlocks were left down and flowing down his back. His eyes, the same color as hers, sparkled, and his gaze landed on her.

He made his way to her and stood before her, a suspicion of a smile on his lips. Kardia grinned and flew into his arms.

"There she is," he murmured, enclosing her into his warm embrace. "It is so good to see you."

She stepped back and waved him into the house. He turned to the guard by the door and gave a slight nod to him. They would be uninterrupted.

"I can't believe you actually came," she said.

Kardia closed the door and found him wandering around the living room. He paused in front of a photograph of her parents, her, and her brother. It had been taken years ago before the night that had changed her life forever.

Kardia tried to not think of the vicious attack she had suffered. A shudder rippled through her at the memories holding off in the distance. She wished to forget that night.

"Of course I would come." He turned to face her.

Wyett Markway was the patriarch of her family. He had been a member of the council for years having inherited the seat from his father, and her father was expected to take the seat once Wyett died. Kardia hoped that day never came. She didn't know what she would do without her grandfather. He had been her rock her entire life. From the moment she was able to walk, she would follow him around. Their bond was strong, and she missed him so much when he was away doing his duty to their people.

"You are my granddaughter. Of course I would come and make sure you are safe."

"Well, I appreciate it." Kardia smiled.

Wyett was the one person who never judged her after that night and had stood by her side even when her own parents stayed away.

Wyett walked over to her and stood in front of her. He didn't say a word as he met her gaze. Her wolf whimpered, sensing her grandfather's beast.

"Can you sense her?" he asked quietly.

Kardia nodded, closing her eyes. She inhaled and focused on her animal. Her wolf hadn't made an appearance in almost ten years. She was broken.

Defected.

An embarrassment to her family.

At least according to her parents. Her grandfather didn't share his son's opinion on her being unable to shift. He had been the one person she could depend on.

"She's there and happy you're here," Kardia said. Her wolf paced back and forth, excited that her grandfather had come to visit. Shame filled her that she wasn't like the other members of her family.

"We won't give up, we'll get you to shift." Wyett said. He rested his hands on her shoulders. His eyes softened, and he leaned forward and pressed a kiss to her forehead. "None of this is your fault."

"I know, Papa," she murmured. She held back the tears that threatened to fall. She sniffed and took a step back. She snagged her bag and put it on her shoulder. "Ready?"

"Yes, we can't leave the alpha waiting."

They exited the house. She locked up her new home and followed Wyett to the waiting SUV. One of the guards stood with the door open. She nodded her thanks to him before crawling in. Her grandfather settled in the seat next to her. Within moments, their caravan was on the road.

"Why the meeting with the alpha?" she asked. When she'd first arrived, she had met with him and his mate. They appeared to be good, caring people. Matter of fact, now that she thought about it, everyone was welcoming. The few times she had ventured out in town, she had felt safe and already part of the community.

"The alpha and I have some business to discuss after a particular event that occurred not too long ago that involved one of his enforcers. Also, he may have someone who can help you."

Kardia didn't want to get too excited. She'd had plenty of people try to help her over the years, and no one was able to draw her wolf out. She leaned her forehead against the window. The beautiful scenery of the woods flew past. She would kill to be able to feel the warm earth underneath the pads of her paws.

Her wolf whined inside her chest. Her beast missed the feel of the sun on her fur, the wind in her face, and the scent of the wild. Kardia had to find a way for her animal to get free. It was as if her wolf was caged inside her and the key was lost.

They continued the rest of the drive in silence. She was happy her grandfather was with her. If he believed the alpha could help her then she would give whoever would try a chance. There was nothing worse for a shifter than being unable to shift.

The SUV turned down a long, familiar dirt road. They had arrived at the alpha's home with the driver parking in front of the beautiful property. Kardia sat up and hefted her purse strap onto her shoulder. A guard opened her door and assisted her from the vehicle. Wyett met her on her side just as the front door of the house opened with the alpha and another man stepping out onto the porch.

"Wyatt, welcome to my home." Evan Gerwulf was a large man whose voice rang out with a deep-rooted authority that even had her wolf sitting up to listen to him. He came down the stairs with his hand outstretched to her grandfather. The other wolf remained on the porch, leaning against a pillar. The two powerful wolves shook hands and slapped each other on the back. It was good to see her grandfather smile. He held such an important position, he was always under a ton of stress.

"Thank you for having me, and again, I must thank you for opening your pack to Kardia." Wyett rested a hand on her shoulder.

Evan's amber gaze landed on her. He offered her a smile and his hand. Kardia waved and took his hand in a firm shake.

"Any member of your family is welcomed." Evan's stepped closer to her.

The waves of his powers washed over her. His wolf rumbled low, reaching out to hers. She smiled softly, sensing her animal submit to his. Her wolf recognized his animal and knew Evan was safe and trustworthy.

Kardia jumped at the reaction her wolf gave.

Her wolf was practically purring her response to the alpha.

Kardia urged her animal to shift.

No. Her animal shrank back.

"I can feel her. She's frightened, and something is still preventing you from shifting?" Evan asked. He stepped back and broke the connection between them.

"I still can't shift. She pulls away from me the moment I mention it or try to get her to come forward," Kardia admitted. She blinked back tears, not wanting to appear weak before the alpha.

"I think I know someone who will be able to help." Evan gave her a nod and turned back to her grandfather. He motioned to the house. "Come. Let's go in and settle down. Your men are welcome to rest and relax. Decker can show them where. We are all safe here."

"You have a lovely home," Kardia said. She faced the alpha's wife, Jena. They had taken a walk along their property to allow Evan and Wyett to have their meeting. The path they were on was lined with beautiful greenery, tall, wide trees that appeared to brush the sky. Kardia lifted her face to the sky and inhaled deeply.

Her wolf sighed, sitting up inside her.

Well, if you came out, then you can enjoy this, she said to her animal.

The wolf had the nerve to snort.

"Thank you. Have you been finding your way around town?" Jena asked.

She was very easy to speak with. Jena had shared stories of her family and friends. Kardia was slightly envious of the relationship Jena had with her kids. It would appear she and the alpha were close to their children. Kardia used to be close with her family. She never thought she would see the day they would be estranged.

"I have and plan to look for a job soon," she said. While exploring, she'd seen many businesses with Help Wanted signs in the window.

"If you need help getting work, just let us know. Evan and I will be happy to make some phone calls." Jena smiled. "Anything that piqued your interest so far?"

"A few, but I'm trying to decide." Kardia had studied to be an engineer at the direction of her parents, but it wasn't something she was passionate about. Now that she was away from her parents, she could see what she wanted to do. As a Markway, she was to be great at something. When she'd been younger, her parents had her tested, and she'd scored at genius level in her studies. Going into engineering was an easy way to get her parents off her back.

But she got no joy from it.

For once she wanted to pursue something that she would be proud to do because she was passionate about it.

What that would be? She had no idea.

"It looks as if their meeting has concluded."

Jena motioned to her grandfather and the alpha who were waiting for them at the end of the trail.

Kardia smiled at the men and made her way to them.

Wyett rested a hand on her shoulder when she arrived.

"Everything good?" she asked. She was curious what the two had to meet about. It had to be important for them.

"Of course, my dear. Evan is a good man, and he will be helping the council with some needs we have." He gave her a squeeze before letting her go. "But you don't have to worry about that. The alpha wants to share with us who he thinks can help you."

"I'm all ears." Kardia exhaled. She folded her hands together and turned her attention to Evan. She watched how Jena leaned into her husband and his arm came to settle along her shoulders. She sighed, seeing how they were bonded together. The love energy that flowed from the two of them was beautiful. Kardia hoped one day she would have someone she could spend her life with.

Fate, unfortunately, hadn't blessed her with a mate.

What she wouldn't give to have someone be presented to her. She hadn't given up on fate giving her someone. Kardia promised herself she would be patient.

"Here in Howling Valley, there is a powerful coven, the White Lotus. Their coven has been around for hundreds of years. I spoke with their priestess, and they want to help."

CHAPTER TWO

"One. Two. Three." River spun around with her hand in the air.

"All eyes on me," the children in her class chanted.

Quietness fell around them. It was time for them to head outside where they got to get creative and have a hands-on experience.

River eyed them all. They had got a little excited and were being kids, but she was entrusted to educate them. This was Magic 101 for the kiddos. Ten bright-eyed seven- and eight-year-olds stood in line and waited for her.

But if they weren't going to behave, then they would have to go to plan B.

And this lesson was to be fun. River held back a smile and lowered her hand. Her kids were great, it was just the excitement of doing their first experiment.

"That's better. Now, I want to give you clear instructions that you have to hear, and if you're talking, then you will miss out on something important."

Nods went around, and her heart melted. These children were all members of her coven, and part of their normal curriculum included learning witchcraft.

River Delacroix was a witch and proud of it. Her family could be dated back centuries and were a vital part of their coven, the White Lotus. Her grandmother was the current serving priestess. Howling Valley was where she had grown up. The town was a mix of humans and the paranormal. One thing River loved so much about Howling Valley was the peace and harmony of everyone who called the town home.

A small hand in the air grabbed River's attention.

"Yes, Winter?"

"We're sorry, Miss Delacroix," Winter said. The small girl with two black pigtails and wide eyes put her hand down. "We'll behave."

The rest of the kids nodded and murmured their agreement.

"Thank you, Winter." River walked over to her desk and motioned to Winter. "Would you be so kind as to help me pass out baskets to everyone?"

"Yes, ma'am." Winter got out of line and came to River.

She handed the little girl ten baskets that were setting on her desk.

River grabbed her sunglasses and moved over to the door that led to outside. She opened it and smiled. The children held their baskets, their faces lined with excitement.

"No running. Don't go too far away from me. Do not go into the woods alone. I should be able to see you at all times." She gave a few more rules and held back a laugh at the dazed looks appearing on their faces. "Okay, let's go. Sam, since you're last in line, please make sure the door closes behind you."

"Yes, Miss Delacroix."

River guided her class outside, and they headed toward the back of the school. There was a small pathway that led them to their destination. The children's excitement was infectious. River loved what she did and wouldn't give it up. Young ones at this age were very impressionable and open to magic. Today, they would learn how to appreciate Mother Earth, identify, and collect their supplies. Once back in the classroom, they would complete their first potion.

They arrived at their destination. Before them were fields filled with bright, beautiful dandelions. River turned to her class and grinned.

She held up her hand, signaling she wanted their attention. Their conversations died down. Gasps went up in the air as they took in the sights before them.

"We are here to gather dandelions," River announced. Before she let them go to gather the yellow flowers, she wanted to throw in a quick lesson. "Does anyone know what a dandelion can mean?"

"Beauty?"

"Love?"

"They taste nasty."

Giggles went around.

"All of you are correct." River laughed. "Dandelions are very helpful. As you grow in your journey to be great witches and warlocks, you will come to understand this plant that many humans believe is a weed. But to our kind, it can be a powerful ingredient when you need to perform spiritual communications, purification, summoning, and healing. Even warding off dark thoughts and other bad things."

River's primary focus was healing. She had studied under her mother and aunt. One of her primary duties in the coven was that of a healer. Teaching was a passion of hers. One summer, the Magic 101 teacher in the elementary school had taken personal leave. River had been asked to substitute, but when the other teacher didn't return, River had stayed on.

After she gave their final instructions, the kids took off running and screaming toward the fields. River remembered being their age and how excited she was in her first magic class. The children scattered along the field, going to work.

The day was perfect with the bright sun high in the clear-blue sky. She couldn't have asked for a better day. The sounds of their laughter and excited chatter filled the air. River pushed her hair out of her face and tucked it behind her ear.

She stiffened, sensing a presence behind her. River glanced behind her and took in her grandmother, Jimma Jinx. Her long gray hair was in a single braid that rested on her shoulder. For a woman who was pushing ninety years old, she didn't look a day over fifty. The elder witch made her way to River's side.

"Ah, the dandelion lesson. This is a good one."

"I learned from the best." River smiled.

She glanced over at Jimma, who was enraptured by the children. Her grandmother loved all members of the coven, but she always had a soft spot for the little ones. The dandelion lesson had been taught to River by her grandmother. River knew she was one lucky witch. She was blessed by the goddess with an amazing family.

"You sure did." Jimma winked at her. "I almost forgot why I came here."

"It wasn't to come visit your favorite granddaughter while she's at work?" River teased.

"That's always an excuse," Jimma said. She reached over and cupped River's cheek. Her smile slowly faded, and the high priestess dropped back and turned her attention back to the munchkins. "I was contacted by Evan Gerwulf."

"The wolf alpha?" River stilled. It had been a while since the alpha had to call on their coven. The last time was when a new witch had blown into town being hunted down by her former coven. Cora Latimer, the mate of Addy Ransome, was a very powerful witch who they'd openly accepted into the White Lotus. Her former priest had wanted to use her powers for black magic, but he had been no match for Cora.

River worked with Addy, who was a third-grade teacher at the elementary school. She was a wolf shifter who was madly in love with her witch.

River had befriended both of them. They were fated soul mates, and anyone within a five-mile radius could see they belonged together.

River bit back a sigh, thinking of the beautiful couple. She prayed to the goddess that one day she would be blessed to meet her special someone. All witches were born with a "knowing" inside them. When their other half was presented to them, they just knew. It was the moon goddess who chose the perfect person for them.

All witches were taught about "the knowing." That conversation was just as vital as the "birds and the bees" chat.

River would be patient and wait for her soul mate to present themselves to her.

"What did the alpha want?"

"There's a new wolf who recently moved to Howling Valley who is in need of healing."

"Healing? But shifters can self-heal with shifting." River was confused. Shifters had unique abilities to heal swiftly unless it was a fatal wound. But this was still an odd request. The shifters also had their own healers to rely on. Why would they need a witch healer?

"That is the problem. The young woman cannot shift, and they are asking for our help with this matter."

River walked into her home and threw her bags down on the couch. She had been anxious for the day to end so she could go home to research. She kicked off her sandals and flew into her spare bedroom that doubled as her office.

To be asked to help a shifter who couldn't shift was an honor. If her grandmother believed she was the witch who could help the poor wolf, then she wouldn't let her or the wolf down.

River took a seat at her desk and booted up her laptop. She would have to do research before she met the wolf. Her grandmother had shared that the wolf was also practically royalty in the wolf shifter world.

"No pressure," River murmured. Once her computer came on, she went online and logged in to The Divinity, a secured message board for witches and warlocks. She wanted to see if there was any chatter of others who may have helped a shifter like Kardia.

River paused, realizing it was the first time she had even said the wolf's name.

"Kardia." River stilled, a fluttery sensation flickering in her belly.

That was certainly weird.

River blew out a deep breath and returned her attention to her computer. She began her search, going through as many message boards as she could.

Her eyes grew tired. She rubbed them for the tenth time in a matter of minutes. River sat back. The room had grown dark. She glanced at the time stamp on the computer screen and saw it was after ten p.m.

"Where has time gone?"

Standing, she stretched out her aching muscles and blew out another deep breath. She had come across a lot of information. There had been documentation of witches who had created potions for shifters who had been stuck as their animals, others who shared stories of uncontrollable shifts, but not much information about being stuck as their human form and not being able to transform into their animals.

River's stomach chose that moment to make itself known. It had been a while since she had eaten lunch, and she now found herself starving. She anticipated a long night ahead of her. She had to keep researching. There had to be something out there that could help her.

River left her office and went into the kitchen. She opened her fridge and didn't really see anything appetizing to eat.

"Microwave dinner it is," she murmured. She pulled open the freezer and took out a random dinner. Once it was in the microwave cooking, she made herself a big cup of tea. She took her meal and drink back in her office.

Her mind was racing with all thoughts and possibilities that she could use to help this wolf.

Blowing on her cup of tea, she thought of the wolf's name.

Kardia Markway.

Kardia was a beautiful name. It was unique, and she'd never heard of it before.

This time when she said her name, her stomach filled with butterflies.

"What does this wolf look like?" River uttered. She sipped on her drink and opened another window on her computer. She typed in the wolf's name, and the screen was flooded with articles and photos of the woman.

River's breath was snatched from her.

Kardia was beautiful. Warm brown skin, big brown eyes. Her dark hair was pulled into an updo, and she was dressed in an expensive ball gown. The picture was captured at a charity ball her family had hosted.

River clicked on multiple pictures, enraptured with what she was seeing.

There was an article with the headline: Wolf in the Shadows. She clicked on the link and began to read. Apparently, there were questions on why the daughter of such a prominent family was rarely seen with them. Kardia was only ever seen at charity events, and that was it. Public moon runs with the pack never included Kardia.

Hmm…maybe because she can't shift, River thought to herself. Or was this not public knowledge? She eyed her food that still had steam floating up into the air and returned to her computer. There were other articles with theories on why the young woman was rarely seen anymore.

River sat back and stared at a picture of Kardia.

She stared into those golden-brown eyes, and her pulse quickened. She swallowed hard and placed her mug on her desk. There was something about this woman, and River couldn't explain her reaction to her. She had seen and been around plenty of beautiful women, but she'd never reacted so strongly.

Her skin tingled, and her nipples grew taut, pressing against her bra, while her clit pulsed. River ran a trembling hand through her hair.

A nervous giggle escaped her. It had been a while since she'd had a sexual partner, and it been at least a week since she had taken matters into her own hands. A shiver coursed through River, and she found herself unable to look away from Kardia.

"Get a hold of yourself," she muttered. She tore her gaze from the screen and focused on her food. She bought it to herself and made a mental note to take care of the needs her body was alerting her to.

She took a bite of her meal, barely able to taste

it. Her eyes were drawn back to Kardia's photo. Her arousal grew painful.

There was no way she could ignore this or put it off. Her body was screaming for a release. River dropped her fork and pushed her food away. She searched and found another photo of Kardia.

Her hands shook as she reached down and tugged her shirt over her head. Her bra was the next item of clothing she had to take off. A moan slipped from her lips once the cool air kissed her pebbled nipples.

"Goddess above." She groaned and cupped her full breasts, massaging them.

She needed more.

River became lost in the quest to have a hard release. Her hands had a mind of their own and traveled down her flushed body. She removed her skirt and panties, kicking them away. She spread her legs wide, propping a foot on her desk. Her hand dove between her thighs.

She cried out when her fingers parted her slick folds and were met with her wetness. Her finger circled her clit, eliciting a moan from her. The small bundle of nerves was swollen and sensitive. River stared at Kardia and strummed her clitoris.

She didn't know what this was, but at the moment, she wished Kardia was here with her.

"This is crazy." River gasped. She was supposed to be researching how she could help a woman, but instead, she was letting herself go to a photo of the woman. "Hmm… Yes."

River sank two fingers inside her slick channel. Her muscles gripped her fingers tight. She fucked herself, thrusting them deep. Her head rested back on her chair, and she basked in the sensations coursing through her.

Her free hand cupped her breast, teasing her sensitive nipple. River whimpered, wishing the woman of her fantasy was here to help her. River craved the feeling of Kardia's lips surrounding her perky nipples. The thought of Kardia's mouth on her pussy had her body temperature rising.

The pace of her hand increased, slamming her fingers deeper. River's breaths were coming in pants. Her hips rocked forward with the rhythm of her hand. Her core clinched down around her fingers. The sounds of her panting and cries filled the air.

She withdrew them from her cunt, driving them to her clit. Sweat coated her flushed skin. Her body trembled with each breath she took. She flicked her swollen nub while she pinched and pulled her nipple.

"Goddess…" Her word ended on a hitch. The desire to climax overcame her. She needed to have her orgasm now.

She pushed her fingers back into her pussy and brought her other hand down. She spread her legs as wide as she could and thrust her fingers inside herself. She focused her other fingers on her clit and rubbed it.

"Oh, Goddess," she chanted. Her body trembled from the power of the sensations rocking her body. A vision of Kardia appeared, and River teetered on the edge of ecstasy.

She pinched her clit, and her body detonated.

"Kardia!" The wolf shifter's name slipped from her tongue. Her muscles grew taut, and she shook uncontrollably. Tears slipped from her eyes from the force of her release. Her fingers, still buried inside her pussy, were snug, the muscles contracting around them.

River slumped in her chair, trying to get control of her breathing. Her skin tingled from the aftermath of her climax. She opened her eyes, and her gaze fell back on the photo of Kardia. Her core pulsated while she took in the beautiful woman.

"What is going on?" River whispered. Her hand was covered completely with her creamy release. Just by staring at the wolf, she could feel her arousal growing again. She brought her hand up and chuckled at what she saw.

River bit her lip and eyed the picture again. The waves of desire filled her. She needed another climax. Standing, she paused first to get her bearings. Her legs were slightly weak. Her body was ultra-sensitive, and she couldn't believe she had just masturbated to the image of someone she was to help. She stood to her full height.

No one would know.

If she was going to go for round two, she was going to need some toys. River took the first unsteady step, then another. She went into her room and flopped onto her bed. She opened her nightstand and dug into her stash of toys.

She would finish her research in the morning. Right now, her body was in need.

CHAPTER THREE

Kardia knelt on the ground in front of the garden in her backyard. It was overrun with weeds. She wasn't sure how long her home had sat vacant before she'd moved in, but the weeds had taken advantage of no one being around.

"But I'm here now and I'm going to have you looking beautiful," Kardia murmured.

She had always had a love for digging in the dirt with her hands. Her old job had never left time for her to cultivate her gardens. She had employed someone to make her property appear decent, but now she was in Howling Valley, she was going to make sure she had time to plant what she wanted in her yard and attend to it.

She reached out and grabbed a hold of the last large weed in her sights. She gritted her teeth and yanked hard. She didn't want it to break off where she would have to dig out the roots. Kardia fell back on her bottom with a laugh.

Success.

The roots were intact.

With a smile, she tossed it into the pile next to her. She peered over at the other parts of the garden that surrounded her home. She still had more go, but that was all right.

She had all the time in the world here in her new town.

There was no issue of trying to avoid the media.

Neither of her parents were around to remind her of her disability, and she didn't have to watch them dote on their favorite child, her brother.

Nope.

Kardia could be herself.

She would even go along with her grandfather's wishes to let this witch try to help her.

Speaking of which, Kardia reached for her cell phone to check the time.

"Shit," she muttered. The witch would be there any moment. Kardia glanced down at her clothes, and they weren't too bad. Dark-gray cotton shorts, a black tank top, and bare feet. Her hair was scraped back into a low ponytail. "This will have to do."

Kardia stood, her ears picking up the sound of a car approaching. Even though she couldn't shift, she still had her other abilities such as enhanced sight, hearing, and scent. The crunch of gravel alerted her the car was in her driveway.

Her wolf stood and whimpered. She anxiously paced back and forth.

Kardia froze in place. Was her animal wanting to meet this witch? She couldn't remember her beast feeling nervous. This was fear, or hesitation, but genuine nervousness, as if she was worried whether the witch would like her.

Why are you worried? she asked her animal.

A snort was the only response.

Shaking her head, she walked around the cabin to meet the witch. Kardia was drawing a blank. What was her name again? It was something unique, and for the life of her, she couldn't remember it.

River, her wolf whispered.

Kardia rounded the corner and took in a small black sedan parked in front of her home. It was empty, and a light floral scent hit Kardia. Her gaze moved to the porch where a slender woman with dark hair pulled up into a messy bun stood knocking at her front door.

Kardia stood frozen, the wonderful scent of flowers floating from the woman.

This must be the witch the White Lotus felt would be able to help her. At the moment, Kardia couldn't think of anything but the beautiful woman in a white sundress. A gentle breeze blew, sending the addictive aroma her way. Kardia inhaled it, and immediately, her gums burned from her fangs trying to break through. She reached up and ran a finger along them, surprised her wolf was showing some kind of initiative.

"Hello there," Kardia called out. She cleared her throat and stood to her full height of five foot three inches. She wasn't the shortest shifter around, but when she was younger, she had always wished she was a few inches taller.

The woman spun around toward her, and they both froze in place.

Mate, her animal growled.

Kardia's eyes widened.

What did you just say? she asked her animal in complete and utter disbelief. She had always dreamed of this moment, but it wasn't supposed to happen now.

Not when she was a defected wolf.

Her wolf whined at the thought of being considered defective or disabled.

Then shift, she demanded. *Now would be the time to come out.* She was practically begging her. Why would fate introduce her to her mate now?

No. Not safe, her beast replied.

What do you mean not safe? she snapped. She was thoroughly frustrated with her wolf. If ever there was a time to break free, it would be now.

"Hello. My name is River. Are you Kardia?" River's smile was blinding. She walked down the stairs and stopped a few feet away from Kardia.

"I am. You're from the White Lotus?" Kardia's voice ended on a hitch. She wiped her suddenly damp hands on her shorts and held one out.

"That I am." River closed the gap between them and took her hand in a firm shake.

A strong electrical current zipped up Kardia's arm.

There was no doubt in her mind that this beautiful woman before her belonged to her.

This was her mate.

"It can't be," River murmured. Her grip on Kardia's hand tightened. Her eyes widened, and she stepped closer to Kardia.

"What is it?" Kardia was just as intrigued with River as she appeared to be with Kardia. River's palm was soft, and Kardia wanted to feel them all over her naked body. River's scent was drawing her to her. Kardia's chest rumbled with a low growl. She closed the gap between them and nuzzled her face into the crook of River's neck. Kardia inhaled sharply, breathing in her sweet aroma.

Her animalistic nature was taking over.

Mate. Claim her, her animal growled.

Kardia was pleased to feel River press close to her.

"Goddess, I can't believe it." River groaned. She wrapped her arms around Kardia's waist, holding her in place.

Not that Kardia wanted to go anywhere. She was right where fate wanted her to be.

In the arms of her mate.

And her mate must be recognizing her for who she was.

Kardia lifted her head and met River's gaze. She took in all of her mate's features and memorized every inch of her face. She was the most beautiful woman she had ever seen.

And she was all hers.

"You are the other half of my soul," River whispered. Her hand came to cup Kardia's cheeks. Her lips curved up into a smile. Her eyes were filled with lust, and she bent down and captured Kardia's lips in a kiss.

Kardia's heart pounded away. She parted her lips, welcoming River's tongue inside her mouth. A moan escaped her. River's tongue stroked hers, teasing her, drawing her deeper into the kiss. Kardia skated her hands along River's body and traveled down to her bottom. Her round ass filled Kardia's hands perfectly. She pulled River close, leaving no space between them.

The feeling of her woman's breasts crushed against hers was wonderful, but to have them naked, sliding against hers, would be divine.

"You can feel this, too?" Kardia breathed.

The moment she tore her lips from River's, the witch trailed hot, openmouthed kisses along her cheek and down to her neck. A moan slipped from Kardia when she sucked on her neck. Her skin was sensitive, and the slow sucking sensation sent a rush of desire to her core. Her pussy grew stick with need for her mate.

The need to strip her clothes off was increasing. She needed to feel her mate's tongue and fingers inside her pussy. Moisture collected between her thighs. Her panties were completely damp.

She had to get herself in control. Otherwise, she'd be having sex for the first time with her mate on the front lawn.

That wouldn't be considered romantic.

But when was a mating between shifters romantic? Must wolves took their mates wherever they wanted. Their animalistic side overcame them. The human in them may want privacy or to plan their mating. The animal in them would throw their mate down wherever they were and seal the bond.

Take her, her wolf snapped.

"River," she whispered.

The witch lifted her head and met her gaze with a lust-filled one.

Kardia couldn't help but press a soft kiss to River's swollen lips. "Come. Let's go to the backyard so we can talk."

River nodded. Kardia took her by the hand, entwining their fingers together. She walked them to the backyard with River right behind her. They moved fast, arriving at the back of the house. Kardia guided River over to the patio where there was few outdoor furniture pieces. She sat on the sofa chair that allowed for two people. River took the spot next to her with a sexy smile on her lips.

"This explains everything," River murmured. She leaned forward and kissed Kardia again. Her hands slid along Kardia's bare thigh.

"What?" Kardia was trying to get control of herself, but it didn't help that River's hands and lips were appearing everywhere. Her lips caressed Kardia's shoulder.

River lifted her head and met Kardia's gaze.

River didn't respond. Her hand had made its way to underneath Kardia's tank top. She had pulled down the cup of Kardia's bra and was massaging her bare breast.

Kardia bit her lip, a whimper slipping from her.

River was bold, drawing Kardia's shirt over her head. Somehow, her bra had disappeared just as quick.

They needed to talk.

Kardia couldn't believe she was about to push River away, but the second River's lips closed around her nipple, all lucid thoughts left her.

"Oh," Kardia breathed. She cupped the back of River's head, keeping her in place.

River's tongue teased her nipples. She slipped from the chair and knelt on the ground in front of Kardia.

"River, we need to talk," Kardia said. She widened her legs to allow her mate to lean in more.

River suckled at her breast while her free hand squeezed and rubbed her other one.

"We will have plenty of time to talk." River's lust-filled eyes glanced up at her. Her finger rotated her nipple before pulling on it slightly. "The urge to taste you is too strong. The knowing is burning inside me."

Kardia had some knowledge of witches and had heard of this "knowing." It was the equivalent of the mating bond flaring to life in a shifter.

There would be nothing to sate the need but a claiming.

"Even though you know I can't shift, you still want me?" Kardia asked. Tears blurred her vision. This was something she had to know. She didn't want to move further if River wouldn't want her as she was.

"Why would that stop me? If you were human, I'd still want you."

River's hands slid down Kardia's body and paused on the edge of her shorts. She tugged on them and Kardia's panties. Kardia rose slightly, allowing River to strip her of the rest of her clothes. River's gaze paused on Kardia's center then flicked back to her. "We will figure this out. Together."

River rested her hands on Kardia's thighs and eased them farther apart.

"Together?" Kardia echoed.

"Yes, together."

Kardia lifted her legs to prop her feet on the edge of the sofa. River smiled and traced Kardia's slit with her finger. She slipped the tip inside River. Kardia whimpered, wanting more. She slid down in the chair, spreading herself open for River. Her breaths were coming in pants in anticipation of what was to come.

River's finger moved up to her clit, drawing circles on her sensitive flesh.

"Yes," Kardia hissed.

"Your pussy is so pretty," River murmured. "Just as I imagined it to be."

She leaned forward and licked Kardia's slit. Her tongue dipped slightly into her channel. Her soft hands rested on Kardia's while she licked her again. Kardia's head fell back on the sofa pillow, and she basked in the sensations coursing through her body.

River's moan floated through the air. She repeatedly dragged her tongue through Kardia's wet slit. She took her time exploring and getting to know Kardia's cunt.

She latched on to Kardia's clit, eliciting a deep, feral moan from her. Kardia's hand flew out and rested on the back of River's head. Her hips gyrated, thrusting her pussy into River's mouth.

Her mate was consuming her, shunting her to the edge of ecstasy. Kardia's hips had a mind of their own. She ground herself to River's face, seeking what she desperately needed.

River sank a finger completely inside her. She arched the finger, fucking her with it.

"Another one," Kardia moaned.

River complied, adding a second. She set a pace that was in rhythm with Kardia's hips, pumping them harder. Kardia panted, her body trembling.

Her breasts grew heavy, her nipples hard as diamonds. She reached up with her free hand and cupped one of her breasts. She pulled on her nipples, the motion sending a shock of desire to her core.

River sucked on her clit, the pressure increasing while she fucked Kardia's channel even harder with her finger. A third finger swept in, stretching her even farther. Kardia cried out, feeling herself slip over the edge. Her muscles grew tense, and her hips thrust forward. River took advantage and hummed while she tugged on Kardia's clit.

Kardia's breath was ripped from her as she flew up into the heavens. Her climax washed over her, her release spilling from her. She flopped back down on the sofa. She opened her eyes and found River's gaze on her. River released her clit and sat back. She withdrew her honey-coated fingers and licked them clean.

"Come here," Kardia muttered. She reached forward and cupped River's face.

Her mate eagerly offered up her lips to her. Their mouths fused into a hot, sultry kiss. The familiar taste of her pussy met her, and it fueled Kardia on.

Her animal snarled, pacing back and forth.

It was time for them to please their mate.

CHAPTER FOUR

River stood and removed her clothing. Kardia's eyes glowed their shifter amber color while she took in River's naked body. She crawled onto the sofa, straddling her soul mate. She leaned forward and kissed Kardia again.

The taste of her mate would be forever burned on her tongue. The moment she had turned around on the porch and seen Kardia standing there, the knowing had flared to life inside her.

This completely explained what had gone down in her home last night. She had stayed up half the night bringing herself to completion. Over and over, she'd climaxed to the mental image of Kardia.

Now that the wolf was in front of her, she gave herself over to the primal need to have her.

Licking her to an orgasm pleased River. She had imagined it last night, and today, it came true. The fantasy Kardia didn't hold a candle to the real woman.

Kardia's hands rested on her back, and their kiss grew. Their tongues writhed over each other. Kardia nipped at River's lips, and she'd then soothe it, then kiss her again. River's hands cupped Kardia's face, tilting her head. She couldn't get her tongue far enough in Kardia's mouth.

Kardia's hands slid along her body, down to her ass. She brought River closer to her.

River lifted on her knees and broke the kiss. She offered her breasts to Kardia who didn't hesitate in opening her mouth. River pushed her mound inside, a moan slipping from her. Kardia's tongue played with her nipple before she suckled it.

"Yes," River hissed.

She focused on the sensation of Kardia licking and suckling her breasts. Kardia moved to her other one and continued feasting on her. River rested her hands on the sofa. She dug her nails into the pillow with each of Kardia's teeth grazing her nipple.

Kardia's hands spread her bottom wide, her finger sneaking in between and reaching her slit. Her finger slowly trailed along her slick labia. River inhaled sharply. Her eyes closed, and her head fell back.

Kardia's finger grew bolder, teasing her entrance. She dipped it in, allowing it to be coated by River's honey. She guided her finger up to River's clit, drawing it back through the collective wetness that settled between her folds. Her finger came to River's anal rim. She traced it, drawing a cry from River.

Kardia's hands felt so good on her. Kardia pressed against the rim, forcing the tip of her finger inside. River automatically leaned forward, presenting herself more for Kardia.

Her mate released her breast and dropped hot kisses on her stomach and side. Kardia shifted River to where both her hands were to one side. She held on to the sofa, and Kardia lifted her higher. Her pussy settled on Kardia's mid stomach. Kardia moved her finger farther into River's dark hole while her other hand arrived at her slick slit. Her fingers drifted between her folds.

River's breaths were coming faster. She gripped the cushion while her soft moans filled the air. Kardia's finger was completely inside her dark channel. River rocked against her hand, fucking herself with it.

"Look at you," Kardia's low voice broke through the lust-filled fog that clouded her head. "You're so greedy."

River nodded, a cry bursting forth when Kardia's other hand strummed her swollen clit. River couldn't do anything but gyrate against Kardia's hand.

Her wolf's sharp fangs nipped her side. She gasped, the pain fleeting.

She wanted more of it.

She wanted to feel her mate's teeth all over her. She shivered thinking of the moment where her wolf would sink her fangs into her flesh to claim her.

A euphoric feeling flooded River's senses, starting at the tips of her toes and made its way to her head. She was overwhelmed by the sensations assaulting her. She gave in to the pleasure that slammed into her. Her muscles clamped down around Kardia's finger. Her body was racked with tremors.

River's climax shook her to her core. She held on to the sofa and rode the waves of pleasure. She floated back down and opened her eyes. Kardia's amber eyes were locked on her.

"My mate," Kardia whispered.

"The other half of my soul." River whimpered when Kardia withdrew her fingers. She wrapped her arms around Kardia's neck and settled down on her lap once again. Her inner thighs were coated with her desire.

River kissed Kardia, happy that she had found the one person who the moon goddess deemed to be hers. Time seemed to stand still. She was lost in the feeling of being in the arms of Kardia.

River already sensed her body heating up again. Their soft kisses and caresses were growing more urgent.

"Come, mate," Kardia said. She nipped at River's chin, then trailed her tongue over her skin to soothe the sting. "Let's go inside."

River nodded, rocking her hips against Kardia. The wolf's eyes blared even brighter. She could see the wolf in her woman. She was going to try her damndest to get that wolf to come out.

R iver inhaled and tried to turn over, but a possessive hand gripped her naked mounds. Her eyes flew open, and she took in her surroundings.

She was still at Kardia's home.

She relaxed back into her lover's embrace. The room was pitch-dark. Nighttime must have fallen. She smiled, remembering how they had come into the cabin and fallen into Kardia's bed. They had spent the day making love, and in between their bouts of orgasms and climaxes, they had talked. River wanted to know everything she could learn about Kardia.

But there were some things that Kardia held back. She didn't speak much about the relationship with her parents or what had happened to cause her wolf to not want to shift.

She wasn't going to rush her. They had the rest of their lives to get to know each other. When it came to mating, the bond was important. The knowing inside her flared to life again. It was demanding she bind herself to this wolf.

Her heart fluttered, sensing her body awakening.

Was life going to be like this forever?

Would she always crave Kardia's touch and kisses?

"I will forever love your scent," Kardia murmured. She closed the gap between them, her breasts resting on River's back. She dropped a kiss on River's shoulder. "Have I not pleased you enough?"

River giggled and covered Kardia's hand with hers.

"Of course you have, but I can't help the way my body responds to you." River turned over and faced Kardia. Her eyes were adjusting to the darkness. She could make out shadows and the shape of Kardia. "And if I recall, you wanted to talk."

Their career conversations had been light and simple. They'd discovered they shared similar interests. They loved the same types of foods, and River was excited that the moon goddess had picked Kardia for her. But Kardia had avoided conversations surrounding what had happened to her and what she thought the reason was for her wolf not wanting to come out.

Their arms wrapped around each other; their legs became entwined together. Kardia's warm breasts brushed River's as they lay in each other's arms. Kardia stiffened for a moment before rolling onto her back and bringing River with her. River tucked herself into Kardia's side, resting her head on her lover's shoulder.

"That I did say." Kardia exhaled.

"If I'm to help you, I need to know everything," River murmured. She ran a comforting hand over Kardia's belly. She didn't want to force her to share her trauma, but River needed to know to in order to figure out a solution to her problem. "Are you able to speak to your wolf?"

With Kardia's hesitation, she figured she would start off with simple questions. River was used to healing visible wounds. Healing someone from the inside was going to be a new challenge for her.

But this was her soul mate, and she was going to help her.

"Yes, we speak with each other, and I can feel her." Kardia's voice was low.

There was so much pain in her words that it put an ache in River's chest. Her mate was hurting. River couldn't imagine not being able to practice witchcraft. It was second nature to her and was almost like breathing.

"What does she say to you when you try to bring her out?"

"No. Not safe."

River paused to process that information. So whatever happened to Kardia made her animal fear being the primary of the two.

"I know I need to tell you what happened. As my mate, you deserve to know why I'm a defective mate."

River pulled back slightly with a gasp. Was that how Kardia saw herself? As a defective wolf?

"Why would you say that?"

Kardia eased her arm from underneath River and sat up, resting against the headboard. She turned on the lamp on the nightstand. Light flooded the room, and River squinted as her eyes adjusted. Kardia's amber eyes held a hint of sorrow in them. River pushed up and settled next to Kardia. She took her hand and entwined their fingers together.

"Because I am. As a wolf, I'm designed to protect my mate, but in this form, how can I do that? I wasn't taught to fight as a human. Protection, hunting, providing for my mate were all lessons I learned as a wolf. I'm useless to you right now."

River brought Kardia's hand to her lips and kissed the back of it. River wasn't raised as a wolf and wouldn't understand the culture as she would her own. But she was willing to learn. They were from two different worlds and if they were going to be together forever, there was one thing they would have to learn.

To compromise.

"I think that is sweet that you want to do all of those things for me, but you do know that I would want to do the same for you, too." She squeezed Kardia's hand. A small smile appeared on Kardia's lips. "And as for protection, I can protect us both. I may be a witch with healing powers, but I can kick some butt with my powers."

"But—"

"No buts. We work together, and I don't want to hear you calling yourself defective. We will figure this out. I have a few ideas and I won't stop until I get to see your beautiful animal standing before me. This I promise."

"What did I do to deserve someone like you?" Kardia reached for River and brought her flush against her. She took River's mouth in a hard, brutal kiss.

River melted against Kardia. She returned the kiss with much fervor and emotions that Kardia poured in it. River moved and straddled her wolf. She pulled back and smiled at Kardia.

Kardia's gaze dropped to River's breasts. A rumble vibrated from her chest, hinting that her wolf was indeed near. The glow in her eyes brightened. River's body grew flush as the knowing flowed to life inside her.

Now wasn't the time to bind herself to Kardia. They needed to focus on getting her well, and once they figured this issue out, there would be nothing stopping River from binding herself to her wolf.

Kardia's hands came to a stop on River's waist.

"You didn't do anything but exist. The moon goddess wrote it in the stars above the moment we were born that we would be together," River murmured. Her hands rested on Kardia's. She guided them up to her breasts, a moan slipping from her the second Kardia cupped them. She loved the feeling of Kardia's hands on her.

At the moment, they would continue to discover everything about each other physically. Whenever Kardia was ready to share more with her, she would be waiting.

But for now, they would give in to their carnal needs to have each other.

CHAPTER FIVE

Kardia walked out into the kitchen and found River standing before the coffeemaker. The scent had Kardia beelining directly to her mate. River stood, dressed in a towel. She appeared fresh from a shower. Her wet, dark hair was slicked back away from her face.

Kardia arrived behind River and wrapped her arms around her waist and pulled her back to her. She nuzzled her face in the crook of her neck and inhaled her fresh scent.

"You showered without me," Kardia

murmured. She nipped River's skin gently, pressing a kiss to the same spot.

"Well, you were sleeping so good, I didn't have the heart to wake you. Plus, I think better in the shower, and I'm sure if you were there with me, there would have been no thinking." River chuckled.

"You know me so well already," Kardia said.

Last night, River had tried to get her to share what had happen to her, but she had frozen. She was embarrassed, ashamed, and afraid that River wouldn't want her after learning what had happened to her. Kardia was still in shock that River would even want her.

She was a wolf who couldn't shift.

She knew after plenty of counseling in the past that it didn't make her any less of a wolf, but still it hurt, and it was very frustrating that she couldn't roam this earth in her animal form.

How would she claim River?

Yes, she knew her fangs were what created the mark and she was to be in her human form anyway, but she didn't want to mate with River if she couldn't bring her animal out. River tried to make her feel better about her situation. She firmly believed she needed to be whole if she were to complete the bond with River.

As much as it hurt her to admit it, she would rather walk away from River than have her bound to a disabled wolf.

She didn't say defective.

Disabled.

She had come to terms with this label.

"Then this is another thing we have in common." River smiled at her over her shoulder.

The coffee pot was almost full, and the aroma filled the room. Kardia inhaled and took in the delicious scent along with another familiar one infusing the air.

"What is that?" Kardia asked playfully. She already knew the answer, but she wanted to see what River would say. Kardia, unable to resist, slid her hand down River's abdomen and slipped it underneath the towel. Her fingers slid along River's mons and arrived at her folds. River's swollen little bud was protruding as if it was waiting for Kardia's attention.

A moan erupted from River. Her head fell back against Kardia's shoulder. Kardia ran her finger along the bundle of nerves and drew small circles around it.

"The coffee," River whispered. Her eyes fluttered closed, and she turned her pleasure over to Kardia.

A growl ripped from Kardia. Her wolf stood at attention.

Bite her, her animal snapped.

Kardia's gums burned and stretched as her fangs descended.

"Just the coffee?" she asked.

She dipped her finger between River's slit and was met with slickness. She gathered some of it and guided it back to her clit. She applied more pressure to her nub while rubbing circles on it. Kardia leaned down and ran her sharp fangs along the delicate skin of River's neck. It wouldn't take much for her to sink her teeth into her mate's flesh.

As much as she desired to bite her, she wouldn't. Her animal was just going to have to understand.

No shifting.

No mating.

This would be as much as a punishment for her as it would be for her wolf.

"No, we both love pleasuring each other." River's arm reached up, and she curled her hand on the back of Kardia's neck. She turned her face, her parted lips seeking Kardia's.

Kardia obliged her and pressed her lips to hers. She could feel the difference of River's body. Her breaths were coming faster, her muscles were tightening, and her hips gyrated against Kardia's hand. The towel slipped from River and drifted down to the floor.

Kardia didn't waste any time using her free hand to cup and play with River's mound. She ran her hand over River's hard nipples. She was learning fast that River loved for Kardia to attend to her breasts. She broke the kiss and licked and nibbled her neck and shoulder.

River was right about one thing.

They both loved giving pleasure to each other.

"Kardia," River moaned.

She rested her hands in the counter. Her breaths were coming in pants. Kardia loved to hear her name on River's tongue. Now she needed to hear her scream it. Only then would she be satisfied since River had denied her the opportunity to shower with her.

Kardia pulled her away from the counter to force her to lean back on her. She sped up her fingers, flicking River's clitoris. She closed her hand around River's breast.

She pinched and tugged on the hard bud. She brought her mouth to River's neck and suckled on her skin. River's body writhed in place. Her moans and cries were the only sounds in the air.

Kardia's wolf paced back and forth. Her beast was paying close attention to their mate.

Bite her, her animal demanded.

No, Kardia shot back to her wolf. A growl poured from her. The wolf in her was pissed. A wave of frustration rippled through Kardia. Maybe River was the key.

"Oh, Goddess," River groaned.

Kardia pinched her nipple, at the same time extracting a scream from her mate. "Kardia."

River's body grew taut as her climax took a hold of her. She trembled and gasped, her body arching from the pleasure. Kardia held her, riding the waves of her release. A moment later, River went lax with Kardia catching her before she folded to the floor.

Kardia softly kissed her shoulder and ran her fingers along River's drenched slit. She murmured sweet nothings to her mate. She made a vow that she would always worship her body.

"I think the coffee is ready." River chuckled.

"It would appear that you are correct." Kardia laughed softly. She kissed River's shoulder before bending down to pick up the fallen towel. She wrapped it around River, helping her tuck it in to keep herself covered.

River spun around to face her.

"Oh, so now you want me covered," she teased. She draped her arms around Kardia's neck, bringing them close.

Kardia growled playfully. She would prefer her woman to be naked, but this would have to do for now.

"Only so you can finish what you were doing." Kardia took advantage of their closeness and pressed a chaste kiss to her lips. She lifted her head and grinned. "If you want me to remove it again, I can."

"Nope." River stepped back from her with a smile on her lips. She held on to her towel as if afraid Kardia would snatch it off. She leaned back against the counter and sighed. "I have an idea I want to try with you, and I mean about accessing your wolf, not sex."

Kardia's smile disappeared. She nodded. Bringing her wolf out was important. She couldn't spend the rest of her life trapped inside Kardia. Her wolf wasn't meant to be jailed up forever. No matter if she thought it was safe or not, her animal needed to be freed.

"Let's go a little farther," River murmured.

She glanced around at their surroundings and drew in a deep breath. When she had woken up that morning, she had felt guilty about slipping out of the bed and leaving Kardia slumbering. She had stood at the edge of the bed, taking in her beautiful soul mate. Her lips curled up into a mother smile thinking of how the goddess herself was a jokester.

The goddess knew she had designed Kardia for her, so she had put her wolf in her path. River searching for the wolf online had led to her finding her picture, and the moment River had seen it, the knowing had flared inside her.

Only River hadn't realized what it was.

She had thought that she was just horny and needed to get herself off, when in reality, her body was preparing her for the moment she would meet her mate.

Even standing over Kardia and watching her sleep, River had become unbearably aroused. She was surprised Kardia hadn't woken up from the scent of her arousal. Tearing herself away from the bed, she had slipped into the bathroom and taken a shower. Until she had bonded to her wolf, she would have these reactions.

Her wolf must have been exhausted to not hear the water running. River had thought to wake Kardia up with a tall cup of strong coffee, but she had never gotten the chance. Her soul mate had found her in the kitchen and gave her another out-of-this-world orgasm.

River stepped out into a small clearing that would be perfect. She took the blanket from Kardia's arms and laid it down.

"You're going to lie here." River motioned for Kardia to get on the blanket.

"Are you going to join me?" Kardia joked. She sat as instructed and turned to River.

"Nope." River tried to fight the grin from forming on her lips. It was hard to stay serious when her mate was in a playful mood. She reached inside her bag that was on her shoulders and knelt on the ground next to Kardia. Placing a few things beside her, she eyed her wolf. "Are you ready?"

Kardia's smile disappeared. She jerked her head in a nod, and it was then that River was able to see the full force of how this had affected her. River reached for her hand and took it between her two.

"Everything is going to be okay. I'm here with you," she assured her. River meant every word she'd said. They would figure this out between the two of them, and if she couldn't, then she would go to every witch she knew to get her mate to shift.

"I know. I trust you."

River's heart pounded. She leaned forward and kissed Kardia's lips, hard.

"Thank you." She lifted her hand and brushed Kardia's dark hair away from her face.

She smiled and motioned for her to lie down. Kardia did that and stretched out her legs, resting her hands on her stomach. She was dressed in comfortable clothing that she wouldn't care if she shifted and it was shredded.

River blew out a deep breath and turned her face to the sky.

Heavenly Goddess, be with me.

She opened her eyes and glanced down at Kardia who had put her utmost trust in her.

River reached for her first item she had pulled

from her bag. It was a carnelian stone. The reddish-orange stone was streaked with some white particles. She held it up to the sky and muttered a few incantations, asking the goddess to bless her hands and her heart, along with requesting the strength for what she was about to do.

River placed the stone on Kardia's chest.

This stone was very important for the process. It was of the earth elements, and what she needed to do was to ground Kardia back to the earth. Her beast needed to feel one with nature again. She was a creature of this wonderful planet, and reconnecting to Mother Earth was necessary.

River stood and picked up the salt at her side. She walked around Kardia and sprinkled salt around her, creating a small circle. She left enough room where she would be able to sit near Kardia's head. This was important, allowing her energy to stay entrapped inside the area and surge into Kardia. She also didn't want any outside interference by anyone who may have used their powers to attack Kardia.

Once she was done, she sat near Kardia's head. She tossed the empty vial aside and turned back to her wolf. Without a word, she dug inside her bag for the last items she needed.

A candle and matches.

She lit he candle and sat it on flat ground by Kardia's knee. The scent of it would allow her to focus on this realm while she tried to help Kardia.

"This won't hurt. I promise," River murmured.

"It's all right. I can handle it if it does," Kardia replied. Her eyes remained closed, and she appeared relaxed. There was a light breeze blowing, and the sounds of nature echoed around them.

River placed the tips of her fingers to Kardia's temples. She exhaled, sending her powers traveling down her arms. Her fingers grew warm, pushing her energy into Kardia. River closed her eyes and allowed herself to give in to what the fates had bestowed on her.

She imagined the flame of the candle in her mind.

The core of the world.

Hot and fiery.

River inhaled deeply, taking in the scent and warmth of the candle.

The aroma of cedar, spices, and sage filled her nostrils.

Soon, a slight spark of electricity hit where her skin met Kardia's. She was connecting with her. She pushed farther, feeling herself tumble down an invisible path that would lead her to Kardia's wolf.

River's eyes flashed open, but she didn't see the woods as they were before she'd begun.

There was no sign of Kardia.

Only the beautiful, lush woods. It was silent. The sounds of nature were no more. It was as if she was in the calm before a storm. Everything remained gorgeous and even serene.

But she knew she wasn't in the same woods that were behind Kardia's cabin.

River remained calm, sensing she had fallen deep into Kardia's psyche. She didn't feel anything that would alarm her. A presence was out there, and River knew, without a doubt, who it was. She patiently waited, a small smile forming on her lips.

She didn't have to wait long.

An exquisite white wolf appeared at the edge of the woods, staring at her. Her amber eyes glowed in the shadows of the trees. The beast was curious, tilting her head to the side.

River offered a warm, welcoming smile. This was the first time she had laid eyes on Kardia's animal.

"I see you," River whispered.

She was captivating.

The wolf cautiously took a step away from the brush, keeping her eyes trained on River. She paused, sniffing the air.

River stood from her perch slowly. Kardia's wolf was massive, standing almost as tall as River. She held her hand out to the wolf, wanting to officially meet the other half of her soul mate. Kardia's wolf was an extension of her, and the animal must accept River.

"Do you know who I am?" River whispered.

The wolf took another step toward her, breathing in her scent. River was certain she saw recognition in the animal's eyes. The beast took another step, then paused. She had traveled halfway to River before her ears perked up.

River glanced around and took in the scenery changing. The lovely landscape melted away, the sun disappearing from the sky that was darkening. Soon, the full moon was high against the dark backdrop. No longer were they in the woods as before.

Now they were standing in the midst of a field. Off in the distance, lights twinkled along the horizon. River squinted, trying to make out where they were.

She blinked, realizing she no longer scented the

smell of the candle that was burning near her body in the other plain.

Her heart rate increased. She wasn't sure if it was hers or Kardia's that she was sensing. The white wolf's ears were pressed down against her head. Her amber eyes flicked to something off in the distance behind River.

She spun around, a gasp escaping her. A dark cloud of energy was racing toward them.

"What in the name of—?" Her words were cut off by the blast of power that hit her.

Dark energy.

It was like nothing she had ever experienced before. She wheeled around, raising her arms to protect her face. The heat from the cloud encircled her. River reached deep inside her and pushed back against it.

A strangled howl rippled through the air.

Kardia.

Something had attacked her in the past.

This was why her wolf was afraid of shifting.

All along, she had thought Kardia had been attacked by other wolves.

No.

This was the work of strong, dark magic.

She had been attacked by a witch.

With River's strangled cry, her energy burst forth from her, creating a barrier around her. She opened her eyes and took in Kardia's wolf lying on the ground. River marched to her, holding her own against the wave of dark magic. She stopped at Kardia's side and knelt by her, bringing her into her cocoon, protecting her from the assault.

Kardia lifted her head, her amber eyes full of fear.

"Don't worry, my love. I will protect you," River vowed. The weight of the dark magic was pressing down on her. She held Kardia's gaze until everything went black.

CHAPTER SIX

Kardia's body trembled. She opened her eyes, hearing River's breaths turn into pants. River's fingers fell away from her head. She was unsure of what had happened, but her wolf inside her grew panicked.

"River," Kardia gasped.

She glanced up at River and found her pale and diaphoretic. Kardia sat up and turned toward her mate. The protective instinct inside her grew strong. She reached out and took River by the shoulders. Her mate's eyes were open, but only the whites showed.

"River."

This time she gave her a little shake.

River blinked, her eyes unfocused.

"Kardia," River whispered. Her hand came up to cup Kardia's face. Her facial features softened as she stared into Kardia's eyes. "I'm so sorry."

Kardia's heart skipped a beat. She cast her gaze down, away from her mate. She wasn't sure what she'd seen, but she didn't want to see the pity in her eyes.

"What are you sorry for?" she asked.

Kardia felt her wolf stand up and push at her stomach. Had River seen the horrors of that night?

River's small fingers tipped her chin up, forcing her to look up.

"I saw your wolf. She's beautiful," River said. Her lips curled up into a smile while fresh tears spilled from her eyelids.

Kardia was unable to speak. She didn't know what to say. It was the first time someone had seen her animal in a long while.

"You don't have to be ashamed of what happened to you," River said.

Kardia blinked.

"What?" Her voice shook. So, River *did* see what had happened to her.

"Someone using dark magic did this to you."

"Can you fix me?" she asked automatically. This was news to her. If River was able to determine this after one time of delving into her memories, then that meant there had to be a solution to her inability to shift. Her wolf could be released again. "Fix us?"

"I will need help, but I know who I can ask. There is a member of my coven who is one of the most powerful witches I have ever known. I'm certain she will assist." River appeared convinced that this person would help a complete stranger.

"How do you know?" Kardia asked. Why would someone who didn't know her, help her? Kardia was a little cautious to seek out someone's help. So many people before had tried to diagnose her or treat her and failed. What made this person special?

"Because Cora is mated to a wolf, Addy. Ever since she joined our coven, we became friends. We can go speak with her."

Kardia sat back on heels. If River trusted this Cora, then she would go to her and see if she could help them. Kardia eyed the candle still burning near them. The scent of it grew stronger with the gentle breeze blowing past them. She thought back to the emotions that had run free in her chest. She'd instantly known the second her wolf had laid eyes on River. She may not have seen what they saw, but she felt the emotions her beast experienced.

Shock.

Fear.

Trust.

Her animal trusted River, and that solidified that this woman was meant for them. Even though her wolf hadn't met her outside of her body, the wolf had the utmost trust for her.

"You think that Cora will know what to do?"

"I do." River took Kardia's hands in hers.

Kardia was immediately comforted by the feel of River touching her. It had been so long since she had felt safe around anyone other than her grandfather. If River believed this other witch could help her, then she would trust her.

"I've seen her do some things that other witches can only dream of doing. It's like the goddess had her hand on Cora."

"Okay, we can go see her." Kardia bobbed her head in a nod. She was willing to do anything she needed to get her wolf out. Her animal paced inside her chest. Seeing River up close and personal did something to her wolf. She couldn't remember the last time she'd felt her become impatient.

Well, just shift, she whispered. Kardia offered control to her beast, but her wolf shook her head.

Disappointment filled Kardia that her other half didn't burst forth from her. Her wolf used to always be excited and immediately take over when Kardia handed off the reins to her.

Don't worry. We're going to get some help. River knows someone who can help us. Kardia refused to give up on her wolf.

"Do you want to tell me what happened?" River's soft voice broke through Kardia's thoughts.

Kardia's gaze flicked to River. Her heart slammed against her chest, taking her breath away. Her hands trembled with the memory of that night.

Tell her, her wolf growled.

She was not going to be able to avoid it any longer.

If they were trying to secure their future and claim each other, then Kardia would have to share everything with River.

The good and the bad.

Kardia moved to sit next to River. The sky was a beautiful shade of blue. No clouds were in sight, and the sun was casting down its warm rays. A gentle breeze blew, caressing her skin softly.

"There's nothing you can say that will change my feelings about you. From what I can sense when I was with your wolf, it was something powerful, dark and evil." River took her hand in hers, linking their fingers together.

Kardia tugged River to her and slid them down to lie back. River snuggled into her arms which gave her a sense of comfort. She tightened her hold on her mate and stared at the cloudless sky.

"My family is well-known. My grandfather, a member of the council. All of my life, I was held to a greater standard than any other wolf. Even more so than the children of alphas. Because of my last name, I grew up sheltered. My parents wanted to direct every part of my life. From the moment I was born, my parents controlled everything: my clothing, when I could be in my wolf form, to what I studied in college."

Kardia paused. It wasn't that she'd had a rough life. She'd grown up privileged and never wanted for anything a day in her life. Their family, a long line of wolves who had served on the council throughout time, was rich and powerful.

For a person looking in from the outside, they

may be envious of her lifestyle, but in truth, she'd basically grown up in a prison.

Happiness and love had never really been included with how she was raised. Something she yearned for and experienced whenever around her grandfather.

"Oh my. Kardia, I'm so sorry." River's hand rested on her stomach.

Kardia focused on the warmth of her palm and placed hers on top of River's.

"Of course, I rebelled at every chance I got, but ultimately, I just gave in. When I went off to college, I studied engineering to please my parents. Unlike my brother, I'm not in line for the council. He's older and is being groomed to be a future council member." Kardia paused, not wanting to think of Ruston. He was older than her by three years, and when they were kids, they had been close. But as they got older, her father drove them apart. Ruston was brainwashed by their father, leaving Kardia to be isolated and alone in their household.

River remained quiet. A soft energy pulsed from her hand, sinking into Kardia. The sensation was warm and comforting. She basked in the energy flowing through her.

"Years ago, things had become heated for my family. The council had made some controversial rulings that affected a lot of packs across the nation. My father called and wanted me to come home."

She remembered that call as if it were yesterday. That day, her father's voice had been different. He'd almost sounded scared, but Kardia figured she had imagined it. There were plenty of times she'd wished her parents loved her as much as they did Ruston. Deaden Markway really hadn't cared about her safety, but he had to make the offer for her to come home. She was sure it was all for show, because of their status in the shifter community. But there was no way she wanted to be under his roof again. Living on her own, she had gained more freedom than she'd ever experienced.

She was a wolf and could take care of herself.

Her father had grown angry when she'd declined his offer.

For the first time, she had been proud of herself for standing up to him. She was no longer a child, and he wasn't going to control her any longer.

"This wasn't the first time my grandfather had been involved in something that pissed off wolves across the country. It's part of his job. There is never a time when any ruling the council may make will satisfy everyone." Kardia shook her head and tightened her hold on River's hand. She inhaled deeply. Diving into past memories was hard, and she had tried to push many of them aside, but her mate deserved to know her background. "That night was a full moon, and my wolf demanded to go for a run. So I did what most wolves do on the full moon, shift and go for a run."

A small smile lingered on Kardia's lips as she continued her story. There was nothing greater than shifting into her beast's body and letting her have control. The magical rays of the moon gave her energy. Her animal was connected with not only the earth but the moon.

The night had been warm with a gentle breeze ruffling the fur on her back while there was not a cloud in the sky. She had stood on all four legs with her face raised to the heavens. The moon's rays caressed her snout and sent a tremor through her. She inhaled, taking in the aroma of nature.

Kardia felt free.

She took off running across the wide-open plains of wilderness. Howls off in the distance let her know she was not alone. She practically grinned and pushed farther. Her wolf relished the open run. She had lost track of time and had finally made it to the mountainous range that was miles from her home.

Kardia was surefooted as she climbed the rocky hill, trying to find the perfect spot to rest. She'd made it halfway up the mountain and found a flat rock to rest on. She sat, panting and loving every minute of it. The scenery around her was something short of heaven. Thick woods, mountains, a beautiful sky, and off in the distance, miles of open land that was home to countless animals.

A howl echoed in the air. Kardia threw her head back and answered the call.

"Arooo…" Her wolf's voice was lovely, holding the note until it was time for her to take in a breath. Kardia paused and listened, soon hearing a different wolf respond. She grinned and leaned down, resting on the smooth surface. Her animal loved to moonbathe. The power of the moon rejuvenated her, giving her strength and a boost of energy.

This was the life.

No responsibilities.

No worries.

Just her and nature.

Kardia's ears picked up on a slight sound of a twig breaking. She lifted her head and turned to look behind her. She inhaled, trying to scent who was near her. Was it another wolf? Had they picked up her location?

She pushed up and turned around, trying to listen to

sense where the sound had come from. The area was thick, the trees keeping the moonlight from entering the space. She sensed a large figure. Something that couldn't be a wolf. Even male wolf shifters didn't grow that big. The hairs on the back of her neck rose. A low growl emitted from her as a warning. She planted her paws flat on the ground, ready to either pounce or run.

The shadowy figure slowly drifted to her. It appeared to enhance in size. A rumble came from that direction, and she squinted, trying to see what, exactly, it was.

Kardia swallowed hard and took a step back. She couldn't go too far due to the edge of the mountain. Maybe settling on this rock ledge hadn't been the best idea. She was now trapped.

A gasp escaped Kardia.

The figure broke through the tree line, and it was a black cloud in the shape of a monster. It spun around and took the form of a wolf, at least three sizes bigger than her. She growled again, wanting this magical mist off of her.

It wasn't fazed by her.

How the hell would she fight a thick mist wolf?

She took a step forward and tried to make herself taller and threatening. Who was controlling this? How was this even possible?

Kardia took her eyes off the shadow for a moment to look at the thin path that was near her that led down the mountain. It hadn't been hard for her to make the trek up, but with a predator behind her, it was quite dangerous.

It was a risk she was going to have to take.

Kardia dashed toward the path but was too late. The thick mist swarmed around her. She howled, the sensations of pain taking over her. Fangs, claws sank deep into her flesh. She fell down on the ground and rolled over, trying to ward off the attack. She snarled and slashed her claws, but it was as if nothing was there.

She yelped as teeth sank into her hind leg. She kicked and rolled back over, coming to stand. She raced forward, but the shadow wolf launched itself onto her back. She tumbled down the hill, locked in terror. Her body slammed into sharp edges of the mountain. She continued her fight, slashing her claws in the hopes that it did something.

Her body landed with a thud on another clearing on the mountain. She stood, free from the shadow. Pain engulfed her. Even though her paws had not connected with the ghostly figure, it had sure done a number on her. Blood seeped from the wounds that lined her body. She swayed and turned around to face the shadow. Her eyes widened at the size of it.

It had grown even larger. The rumble from it shook the ground. She stumbled and tried to straighten her footing. Kardia glanced around frantically and took in a path that led into the woods.

It was either that, or finish falling down the side of the mountain.

She took off along the path, the shadow wolf's howl sending tremors down her spine. She pushed herself as fast as she could. The pain was unbearable, but she had to keep going. Beams of moonlight broke through the trees, providing her with little illumination.

Her heart raced, her breaths coming in pants. She skidded to a halt as darkness surrounded her. She blinked, thinking her eyes were playing tricks on her, but she couldn't see anything.

She spun around, her heart all but leaping up into her throat.

The sounds of the forest were obsolete.

A deep growl rumbled behind her. Kardia turned to face whatever was coming for her. An invisible force slammed into her, and everything ceased.

K ardia blinked, bringing herself back to the present. Her vision came back into focus. She had been so lost in retelling her story that she hadn't realized River had shifted away from her and was leaning on her elbow. Tears streamed down River's face.

"They told me they had been looking for me for five days." Kardia cleared her throat. She had been unconscious for a while. None of her family's healers had a clue as to why she was in a coma.

"Oh my," River's voice shook. She reached out and took Kardia's hand in hers. "I'm so sorry."

"It wasn't your fault." Kardia sniffed. She blinked again to try to clear the tears that banked on her eyelids. It had been a while since she'd allowed herself to fully remember that night. Apparently, her wolf wanted River to know and had tried to share with her what had happened.

"Do they know who did this?" River asked.

"No one believed me when I told them about the shadowy wolf." Kardia barked a harsh laugh. She leaned on her back and rested her folded hands beneath her head. She stared at the sky and tried to push down the hurt that was resurfacing. "Everyone told me that there was no such thing and that my brain was creating a tale due to the trauma. So I finally gave in and told them that there were many wolves. My wounds certainly backed up that theory. And ever since then, my wolf has remained inside me, too afraid to come out."

The tears finally fell. Warm trails trickled along

her skin and disappeared into her hair. River slid next to her, wiping the wetness away.

"You are not crazy. What you saw was real," River whispered. "I saw it, and that was the work of a very powerful witch or warlock. Someone wanted you dead and wasn't planning on leaving proof. This is a curse. An old powerful one that will forever haunt you unless we can break it."

CHAPTER SEVEN

"Cora and Addy are out of town but will return in two days, we can stop by then." River hung up the phone and turned to face Kardia.

Her wolf sat on the couch, quiet. She hadn't said much since they had returned inside. River moved over to her and sat next to her.

She took Kardia's hand in hers, slotting their fingers together. "Are you going to be okay?"

Kardia nodded. "You're the first person to confirm what I saw. For years I doubted myself. I began to believe what they told me." She snorted.

"We are going to get to the bottom of this, and

once we do, you won't have to worry about anything." River squeezed her hand. She sent a quick prayer up to the goddess that she wasn't making any promises she wouldn't be able to keep. River refused to believe the goddess would give her the perfect mate, only to snatch her away. "Why don't we go get something to eat. I can take you to the best diner, and the food will definitely distract you a little bit."

River smiled and stood, tugging on Kardia's hand. Her wolf hesitated before standing.

"I don't know if I'm going to be good company —"

"What are you talking about?" River's voice grew husky. She closed the gap between them and cupped Kardia's cheek. Her mate leaned into her touch, a low growl emitting from her chest. River leaned in and kissed Kardia's soft lips. "You are the perfect person to spend my time with. Come, let me feed you. We can walk around the town and get some fresh air."

"Or we can stay here and enjoy each other's company." Kardia's hand rested on River's waist. Her fangs peeked from underneath her lip.

River's heart skipped a beat at the sight of the sharp fangs.

What would it feel like to feel them sink into her flesh? A shudder rippled through River's body at the thought. She bit her lip and shook her head.

"Oh, no. You aren't going to change my mind. I know great diner we can go, and I promise, you will feel better after you have belly full of good food." River stepped back, breaking their connection. She laughed, watching Kardia roll her eyes.

It was almost too easy to give in to the temptation of sliding back into the bed with Kardia. She grabbed her bag and hoisted the strap onto her shoulder and walked toward the door.

"Okay," Kardia grumbled. She disappeared into the bedroom, returning with her wristlet and keys.

River's heart swelled with an emotion she was quickly learning was love. They were going to have to solve this inability to shift issue really soon so they could bond.

The knowing was demanding it, and it was getting harder for her to resist the temptation of binding herself to Kardia.

River spun around and opened the door, walking outside before she changed her mind and took Kardia up on her suggestion.

The ride into town didn't take long. River loved

having Kardia inside her car. Even with the windows rolled down and the air blowing inside, she still picked up Kardia's scent. It was a mix of floral and the outdoors. River inhaled and had to keep from fidgeting in her seat while she drove. She was trying to concentrate on driving, but the urge to give in to her carnal desires was growing.

"I thought you were wanting to eat?" Kardia asked. She turned away from the window and leveled River with her gaze.

River coasted up to the stop light at the corner and pushed her sunglasses to the top of her head. She smiled and tried to appear innocent.

"What are you talking about?" she asked. Her core pulsed as Kardia settled a hand on her knee.

"The scent of your arousal is growing." Kardia flashed her a fangy grin. Her amber eyes narrowed on River. "I'm sure we can pull over somewhere and we can take care of it, if you like."

As tempting as her offer was, River shook her head. "Nope. I promised you food. We're almost there."

The light turned green, giving her an excuse to tear her eyes from Kardia. She pressed her foot on the pedal and guided the car along. She wasn't going to admit she was thinking of places they could park and have some alone time.

River found a parking spot a few doors down from her favorite diner. She killed the engine and pointed to the restaurant. Tina's Diner had been a staple in Howling Valley for years, and she was thrilled to be able to introduce Kardia to the best cooking in all of California. River would have to admit she ate at Tina's at least once a week.

"We are here."

Kardia's stomach chose that moment to announce itself. They chuckled and exited the vehicle.

"I guess I am hungry." Kardia's sheepish grin was too cute.

River jogged around the car and came to her side. She took her hand in hers, entwining their fingers together. The day was beautiful with the sun high. It was warm with a gentle breeze, and she was walking down the street with the one woman who was meant for her.

"Me, too. It would seem we have worked up an appetite." Between the sex with Kardia and using her powers, River was quite famished herself. Her core clenched at the low growl that rumbled from

Kardia's chest. She pressed a quick kiss to Kardia's lips, then tugged her along.

They quickly made it to the diner and went inside.

"River!" Barb's voice rang out.

"Hey, Barb." River waved to the waitress who was wiping down a table.

The older woman had worked at the diner for as long as River could remember.

"Go ahead and pick your table. I'll be there in just a second," Barb said. She was a pleasantly plump older woman, whose smile was infectious. She had a way of making everyone feel like family the moment the stepped foot through the door.

"Thanks!" River scanned the restaurant that only had a few patrons in it. It was midday, and the lunch rush must not have arrived yet. She guided them over to a booth and slid in next to Kardia. River took her bag off her shoulder and dropped it on the seat beside her.

"You come here often?" Kardia asked, reaching for a menu that was on the table.

River leaned against her, laying her cheek against Kardia's shoulder to look at it with her. She needed to touch her somehow.

Kardia's hand rested on her leg.

The feeling must be mutual.

"I do. I usually just go for the daily special."

"Well, who do we have here?" Barb arrived at their table.

River quickly did introductions.

Barb's face softened as she smiled at Kardia. "Welcome to Howling Valley. If you are a friend of River's, then you are certainly a friend of mine."

"Thank you." Kardia relaxed and smiled.

"And from the looks of it, you two appear to be more than friends." Barb winked at them.

River's face grew warm. There was nothing that Barb didn't pick up. She always had a knack about sensing things in people. River wondered if the woman was an empath.

"Barb." River chuckled.

"Oh, you know I'm just playing with you." Barb winked. She took their drink order and promised to grab their food order when she returned.

"I like her." Kardia patted River on the knee.

"She is special." River raised her head and motioned to the menu. "Have you thought of what you want?"

Kardia turned back to the menu and eyed it. She snagged her bottom lip with her fangs, and it had River wanting to lean in and take that lip between her own teeth. Her breath caught in her throat as she watched Kardia ponder over the menu. She propped her chin on Kardia's shoulder again and inhaled her scent. She closed her eyes and thanked the goddess for putting Kardia in her path.

"I think I'm going to go with the daily special," Kardia announced.

"Sounds like a winner. River, you, too?" Barb breezed back to their table, setting their drinks down in front of them.

"You know me well, Barb," River said, lifting her head. She was an easy customer, and the cook in the back hadn't let her down.

"That I do, my dear. You've been coming here since you were a kid." Barb took their menus from the table. She glanced over at the register by the counter and waved. "I'll be right over, Tom."

"As long as you're in business, I'll be here."

"Let me go put in your order and get Tom out of here. If you need me, holler." Barb gave them a nod and headed toward the front of the restaurant.

River picked up her straw and took the paper off before placing it into her cup. She took a sip of the lemonade and sighed. The tangy, sweet drink was made fresh daily. It was one of her favorite drinks to order.

Kardia sipped on hers and glanced around the diner. It was an older place that the owners hadn't wanted to update. They wanted to keep the old-world charm of the early twentieth century.

"I've heard good things about Howling Valley, about how well it's integrated with humans and those like us," Kardia murmured.

River felt pride when she thought of her town. It was a peaceful area run by the wolf alpha and his pack. It was one safest places to live and raise a family. Her stomach clenched at the thought of children. She'd always wanted to have kids but had wanted to wait until she had found "the one."

But would Kardia want a pup or two?

Things between them had moved fast, which was how it was in their worlds. They acted on the desires of the flesh and that of fate. They hadn't had a conversation of the future and what it would entail. Where would they live? Her home was big enough for the two of them, but was it large enough for a family?

River sat back and was unsure of when she should bring up these questions. It was a chat they needed to have, but she wasn't sure if this was the best moment.

Their food arrived, and River decided to wait. They had plenty of years to think of family and the future.

One step at a time.

"Oh my." Kardia raised her head, her eyes wide as she turned to River. She finished chewing and smiled. "I see why you come here faithfully."

River bounced around in her seat, happy her mate liked the food. She envisioned the two of them coming here frequently. Even meeting friends here, bringing their future children. Tina's Diner would always hold a special place in her heart.

"I told you it was good." River stabbed her fork into her food, lifting it to her mouth. She sighed, enjoying the flavors that burst free on her tongue.

They enjoyed their meals in a comfortable silence.

An idea popped up in River's mind.

While she waited for Cora to return home, there was a few things she could do to protect Kardia. If a witch or warlock had cursed Kardia, then River could do something to protect her.

"When we're done here, I need to make a stop," River announced.

"That's fine. Not like I have anything else to do." Kardia chuckled. She reached for her drink and paused. She didn't move a muscle while she scanned the room. A low growl vibrated from her chest. One of the other patrons turned to glance at her as if sensing her wolf's growl.

"What's wrong?" River asked. She closed the gap between then, laying a hand on Kardia's outstretched arm. She looked around the diner and didn't see anything suspicious.

"I don't know," Kardia whispered. She took a sip of her drink and placed the glass back down on the table. "I just felt a sudden rush of heat through me."

An icy chill slithered through River. This wasn't good.

"We need to leave."

CHAPTER EIGHT

Kardia wasn't sure what had come over her at the restaurant. A warmth had spread through her that was so hot, it had her sweating. Her wolf cowered back in a corner, and Kardia knew this definitely wasn't good.

"Where are we going?" Kardia asked. She walked alongside River to her car.

"There's a few items I want to pick up on the way to your house." River's worried eyes turned to Kardia.

Her mate must have sensed the fear in her and took her hand. Kardia allowed River to guide her over to the car. They reached the passenger door just when Kardia's knees gave out.

She cried out, falling against the car.

"What is it?" River's reflexes were quick. She was able to catch her before she hit the ground.

Kardia's breath was snatched from her. She struggled to draw in a new breath. Her vision waned, going black for a moment. River cursed and was able to rest Kardia against the vehicle.

The forest from that night appeared.

No! she screamed out in her mind. There was no way she could be seeing this. She was just awake and walking to River's car. Fear gripped her as the sight of the mystic figure formed before her.

"Kardia," River exclaimed. Her warm hands cupped Kardia's cheeks. "What is it, babe? Talk to me. Tell me what's wrong."

She concentrated on the feeling of River's hands on her skin.

Kardia blinked, the vision slowly dissipating. She inhaled deeply, feeding her starving lungs. Her gaze met River's, and tears formed in her eyes.

It wasn't real.

She was here with River.

But it had felt as if she had been transported right back there.

"I'm not sure. I've never had this happen before," she admitted. Fear gripped her. For years nightmares had plagued her, making her relive the attack repeatedly. It wasn't until the last year or two she'd been able to block it out and push it away.

But this was new.

It was as if the nightmare was taking over her.

While she was awake.

"Get in the car." River brought her forward to allow her to lean slightly against her while she opened the door. She assisted Kardia in.

Kardia was glad that her mate was with her. She felt so weakened, her knees barely able to hold her up. Had she not been there, Kardia was certain she would have landed on the ground.

River reached inside the car and grabbed her safety belt, securing Kardia. She pressed a kiss to Kardia's cheek before shutting the door. She jogged around the car and slid into the driver's seat.

"Look at me," River demanded. She took Kardia's hand and brought it to her mouth. She kissed Kardia's knuckles, covering her hand with hers. "It was not real. I don't know what you saw or where you went for that brief moment, but it was not real. You are here with me."

"I felt your hands on my cheeks. Your touch

anchored me to you," Kardia breathed. She reached for River and brought her to her. She captured her lips with hers. The kiss was frantic and desperate. She didn't know what would have happened had River not been there. Would she have succumbed to the vision?

River returned the kiss with the same amount of passion and fire.

"I'll always be here for you. Now that we've found each other, I will never let you go." River rested her forehead on Kardia's.

Their heavy breathing was the only sound in the car. Kardia eased back slightly and took in her mate's swollen lips. Her gaze dropped down to the base of her neck where her mark should be.

River's pulse raced. Kardia sensed her blood flowing through her veins.

Determination filled her.

She needed to claim her mate.

As a whole shifter, not some wolf who couldn't take the form of her beast.

"If you think I'm letting you go anywhere, you are mistaken," Kardia murmured. She blew out a deep breath, feeling close to herself. Inside River's car she felt safe, but she was now afraid that whatever that was would return.

River drew away from her, and as much as she wanted to continue holding her, she had to let her go.

For now.

"Well, I'm glad we agree on one thing." River started her car and pulled out into traffic. "This just proves what I had feared."

"What might that be?"

"That whoever placed this curse on you may not be done with you yet." River's worried eyes glanced at her then focused back to the road.

Kardia had never thought of it as being a curse before. She just felt that her wolf may be traumatized by the attack and would one day decide she was ready to come out. Calling this a curse was next-level craziness.

"Curses can be broken, right?" Kardia asked. She stared out the window and watch the scenery of the small town fly past.

"Most of them," River answered.

It wasn't what Kardia wanted to hear. She needed to hear that all could be broken, but she knew that wouldn't be reality.

How had her family not known this was a curse?

She was going to have to contact her grandfather and tell him of River's revelation.

"And you shouldn't tell anyone yet about me thinking it's a curse," River said. She slowed down the car and made a turn at the corner. Her knuckles were white from her gripping the steering wheel.

"Why?"

"I mean, don't tell anyone until we've spoken to Cora. She will definitely be able to tell if it is a curse. What kind of magic it was and if it's breakable."

"Can't we go to your high priestess? Isn't that your grandmother?" Kardia stared at River. Why wouldn't they go to her with their problem? She was the leader of their coven. She certainly should be able to help them instead of waiting two days for another witch to arrive home.

Was River not wanting her to meet her family now?

Because of her problem?

Pain rippled through her chest at the thought that her mate would be ashamed of her. Kardia bit her lip, feeling that familiar emotion come into play.

Self-doubt.

"I hate to admit it, but Cora is more powerful than my grandmother." River glanced over at her and frowned. She guided the car into a parking spot along the street in front of a building. She killed the engine and focused her attention on Kardia. "Don't go getting some crazy notion in your head that I'm ashamed of you or some crap like that."

Apparently, her mate could read her mind.

"Can you read—"

"No, I can't read minds, but it was all over your face." River reached for her hand and tugged Kardia to her.

Kardia leaned on the console and met her mate halfway. River placed a small kiss on her lips, without breaking eye contact.

"You are my everything. My life will center around you. I'd bind myself to you now if you'd let me, so don't get any whacko thoughts that I don't want to show you off to the world."

"I'm sorry. I'm just used to everyone treating me different ever since I haven't been able to shift."

"Well, I'm not everyone. I'm your mate. The goddess designed you specifically for me, and if she meant for us to meet at this moment in our lives, then that means I'm the perfect person for you."

River's lips spread into a wide smile. Her face lit up bright as she watched Kardia.

Her mate was certainly a wise one.

She was right. Fate had brought them together at a time where it mattered the most. She may not be able to shift, but even her animal felt the pull to claim River.

"You're right," Kardia admitted.

River's smile grew even wider.

"And once I get a chance, I'm going to tame my mate and coax her out of you." River dropped another kiss on Kardia's lips before moving away.

Kardia watched her step out of the car, and her own lips curved up into a smile.

Little did River know, she had already begun to tame her and her wolf. Her wolf was practically putty in her hands anytime she was around. She just didn't know it yet. Kardia couldn't wait for the day when her beast and mate could officially meet in person.

Kardia exited the car, shutting the door behind her. She took in the building and saw the name Rapture on the sign above the entryway. Kardia could feel the magic streaming from the store. The windows were covered with lace curtains, and there was a sign advertising a psychic medium.

Maybe this person could delve into her psyche and figure out what was wrong.

"It shouldn't take long to grab what I need." River walked over to the door and stopped, waiting for Kardia. She eyed her, worry filling her eyes. "Are you feeling okay? Do you want to wait in the car?"

Kardia's wolf stood at attention. She didn't like the thought that their mate thought she was weak. They were stronger than they looked. Kardia inhaled and felt like herself. Her wolf gave her a nudge to urge her on.

"I'm good." Kardia smiled and followed River. The hairs on the back of her neck rose. Sweat beaded out on her forehead.

What in the world?

River pushed open the door and went in. Kardia shook her head. Whatever it was, maybe this was residual from the incident. Her wolf faltered inside her, and Kardia held on to the doorframe when she entered the small establishment. Her gaze landed on the rows of shelving in the store, but her vision blurred.

A warm rush of energy slammed into her.

Kardia gasped, her knees giving out. Pain

exploded from her knees when they met the hard floor.

"Kardia!" River shouted.

She rushed back to Kardia who was having a difficult time breathing. The energy had a hold of her. Sharp pinpricks scattered along her arms. She grimaced from the pain that racked her body.

"What is it?" River asked.

"I don't know." Kardia gasped. This was different from when she'd almost passed out at the restaurant. There was no vision, just pain, as if someone were shooting needles and darts at her.

Get out of here, a sharp voice whispered in her head.

She backed her way out of the door and tumbled out onto the sidewalk. Immediately, the pain lifted. She gasped again, staring wide-eyed at the store's doorway. A woman raced up behind River.

"What's going on?" the newcomer asked.

"I don't know." River arrived at Kardia's side. She lifted Kardia slightly, cradling her head in her lap. "We were coming to purchase a few things, but the moment Kardia entered the store, this happened."

"Who's your friend, River?" The woman stared at Kardia with an unreadable expression. She folded her tattoo-covered arms in front of her. Her dark hair was pulled up into a bun on top of her head.

"Kira, this is Kardia, my soul mate." River brushed Kardia's hair from her face. "Kardia, this is Kira, the owner of Rapture."

Kardia nodded. She sat up with River's help and held back a grimace. This was a little embarrassing, falling out twice in one day. No wonder her mate thought she wasn't strong enough and should wait in the car.

Kardia tried to stand, but Kira's words had her freezing.

"My shop is warded against dark magic and, River, your mate is covered in it."

Kardia shivered, holding the warm cup of tea in her hand. She sat at a round table in a room at the back of Rapture with Kira and River. She closed her eyes and blew on the strong, hot brew. She was in disbelief at how robust this curse was. Who would do something this horrific to her?

What had she ever done but try to appease her family and live her life?

Thankfully, Kira was able to chant a spell around her that allowed the store's wards to ignore her. Without that, she wouldn't have been able to step foot in it without being attacked again. Now they were in the back room where the psychic read people's fortunes. The room reminded her of something off the movies with a big round table covered with a black tablecloth, dark blackout curtains over the windows, and a large candle in the middle of the table.

"Whoever cast this spell is very strong," Kira said. She lifted her mug and motioned to Kardia.

"I know. I've spoken with Cora, and she's going to help us when she returns. I wanted to pick up a few things because I was going to put up a ward of protection around Kardia's property." River reached over and patted Kardia on the knee.

The slight movement brought comfort to Kardia.

"I need to speak with my grandfather. Maybe he can shed some light on this," Kardia uttered. She dare not call her parents. They would be of no help and would probably blame her for this. When anything had gone wrong in her life, they always made her contemplate what she did to cause it and how she should have avoided conflict.

The night of her attack, they'd tried to convince her that she should have run somewhere else. That she had secluded herself, and because of that, the attack was her fault.

She sniffed and held back tears. Now was not the time to delve into the family trauma that had haunted her.

"What is it?" River's worried eyes met her.

Kardia attempted a small smile but failed. She blew out a deep breath and gripped her mug tighter.

"Nothing. I was thinking of the attack and how there were some who said I brought it on myself." Once they had entered the shop, River had brought Kira up to date on who Kardia's family was, on her attack, the curse, and how she was charged to help Kardia.

"What reason would you have to want to be cursed and not be able to shift?" River snapped.

Her witch was becoming very protective of her, and it brought on a warm, fuzzy feeling inside Kardia. Her wolf loved the possessiveness her mate displayed, too. Her animal whined, standing and head butting Kardia.

Kardia held her breath. It was as if her animal was wanting to come out. It had been a long while since she had felt her wolf desire something on the outside.

Do you want to come forward? she asked her animal. She exhaled, waiting for an answer, but her wolf remained silent. She turned her attention back to the conversation.

"None. I wasn't involved in any of the politics amongst my people. I stayed to myself, only attending functions that were required of me, and I enjoyed being involved with my community." Kardia loved anything that had to do with charity. That's when she'd volunteered for family duty. She thrived when around her people, and especially the pups. She had a soft spot in her heart for children.

Kardia supported fostering initiatives when it came to parentless shifters. No matter what kind of animal, all children deserved loving homes. Kardia had been active with one of the programs that allowed shifter kids to be adopted by any shifter. Wolves to bears, lions to tigers. It didn't matter. A loving home was more important than the youth living out on the streets with no supervision.

"Whoever has an issue with a hardworking woman, who loves her community and volunteers to find foster kids homes, has a special spot waiting for them in one of the seven hells," Kira muttered.

"Agreed," River said.

"No one is getting sent to Hell." Kardia chuckled, trying to make light of the conversation. She set her cup down on the table and settled back in her chair. "I don't care about the reasoning. I just want this curse lifted so I can shift into my wolf and be able move on with my life."

Kardia was tired of the fear that had lived inside her all of these years. Now that she'd found her mate, she wanted to do what all wolves do when they have their mate in front of them.

Claim them.

"Speaking with your grandfather may help us pinpoint who would want to do something like this to you," Kira said. "Now that you know it's a curse, then maybe he can guide us in the right direction of who may have done this."

"My grandfather had searched under every rock trying to find who did this, but now that we know it's a curse from a strong person who can wield magic, this changes everything." Kardia glanced around the room, meeting both of their gazes.

Her grandfather was the one person she knew

she would be able to count on to help figure this out. Hope blossomed in her chest, but she didn't want to believe too much in it.

What if they can't reverse this curse?

"I'm going to do all that I can," River swore.

"I'm in, too. This was dirty work by someone who needs their ass kicked." Kira snickered. She pushed back from the chair and stood. "Let's go pick out everything we need. I'll help you with warding Kardia's property."

"Thank you. This really means a lot to me." Kardia stood on shaky legs. She'd never had people who were ready to go to bat for her before besides her grandfather. This was a new feeling for her, and she didn't know what to do.

Moving to Howling Valley had been the best decision.

"No need to thank me. Not only are you the soul mate of one of my coven sisters, but it is the right thing to do," Kira said.

River moved closer to Kardia and took her hand, their fingers slipping between each other. She offered Kardia a smile and squeezed her hand.

"Us witches stick together. A threat against you is a threat against us."

CHAPTER NINE

Kardia settled on the steps of her cabin with her cell phone in her hand. River and Kira had disappeared around to the back of the property. She stared down at her phone, trying to figure out how to tell her grandfather that the problem wasn't her. This was the first time she had received news that didn't make her sound crazy.

She dialed his number and waited for him to answer. She didn't have long to wait; his deep voice filled her ears.

"Kardia, my child. What do I owe the pleasure of your call?" The background noise suddenly cut silent. He must have gone to a private room and shut the door. "Is something wrong?"

"Hey, Papa." Just hearing his voice gave her a warm, tingling feeling inside her. Even though he had recently visited, she was desperately missing him already. "I was calling for a couple of reasons."

"This sounds serious, Kardia," her grandfather said, his voice lowering.

"You remember the witch the alpha wanted me to work with?"

"Yes."

"Well, she figured out why I can't shift."

"It's not due to PTSD like all those healers had said before?" he questioned. Her grandfather had had multiple healers and even human doctors assess her, trying to help her. All of them came back to that it was a mental block due to the attack. She'd seen psychiatrists who all felt that eventually her animal would just come out when she was good and ready.

But years had gone by.

"Not even close," she breathed. She shut her eyes and shook her head. "There is a curse on me, preventing me from shifting."

He released a muffled curse. If their conversation wasn't so serious, she would have laughed at him trying to stop her from hearing him use swear words.

And to think she was thirty-six years old.

"How certain is she?" he asked.

"One hundred percent sure." She went into the short story of what had happened to her when she'd tried to enter Rapture. Kardia blinked back tears. As much as she wanted to hound on the question of why her, she needed to focus on how to get this curse off her.

"Oh, baby girl. I'm so sorry," her grandfather's voice grew gruff.

Tears flooded her vision. She blinked them back, but still one trailed down her cheek.

Wyett cleared his throat, his voice returning to the strong, deep baritone she was used to. "Does she have any clue on who could have done something like this?"

"We were hoping you would be able help us on this."

"You think it could have been because of me?"

"Papa, you know I don't bother anyone. I keep to myself. My entire life I've had to adhere to certain rules, go to the best schools, show my face at certain events, get an honorable job all because of my last name. It has to be something that has to do with our family. What happened ten years ago?"

"Ten years ago, I…" He paused and exhaled.

"What is it, Papa?" She pushed up and stood to her feet. Her stomach knotted while she waited for him to continue.

River and Kira came into view. They were in a deep conversation as they carried on toward the middle of her front yard. Her gaze trailed her mate's body, but she shoved all the carnal thoughts that appeared out of her head.

This was not the time.

"Kardia, you have to understand that I am a very powerful man, and with that power, I have to make certain decisions."

"Like what?" She didn't think she was going to like his answer. The knot in her stomach grew.

"I'm charged with not only making decisions for our kind, but for our family as well."

"What did you do?" she whispered.

"I didn't do anything, but I fear that the decision I made put you in harm's way."

"Papa." Kardia locked her knees together to keep them from shaking. Apparently, she was double cursed. Once by some unknown magic wielder and then also because of her last name.

Everything always boiled down to who she was.

"Ten years ago, I was to name two successors. One who would take my place when either I die or step down. The other was for a secret council that was being created. The council wanted to have checks and balances. Should the primary council grow to be too powerful or put our people in danger, the second one would hold power…" His voice died off.

"What kind of power?" This was all news to her. She had never heard of this backup council. What did that have to do with her?

Her heart skipped a beat.

No.

He wouldn't.

"To overrule the primary council. In a sense, the second council would eliminate those who endanger our species."

"And whose name did you give for the second council seat?" Kardia froze. She squeezed her eyes shut and shook her head. Her grandfather wouldn't do what she expected he had.

"Yours."

"Does my father and brother know?" she asked, but she already knew the answer. Her body trembled with the realization of what this meant.

"Your father knows."

"Then they all know," she whispered. Something like this wouldn't be kept a secret from her mother or brother. No wonder they all treated her the way they did. They couldn't outright kill her. Her death would draw too much attention to the family, but if they found a way for her to remain away from the public, then people would forget about her. "Does he know that you hadn't told me about the second seat?"

Her grandfather's silence answered the question.

They knew her grandfather hadn't told her. So they thought to keep something this important as a secret.

"Your father is my heir. He automatically gets my seat. When we designed the second council, we truly hoped that it would never have to be used."

"My brother would want that seat. He would never go against my father. He's one and the same as my father." If the council truly felt they needed a fail-safe to protect the wolf shifter race, then her brother would be the worst prospect. He was just like her father and would ensure his wishes would be carried out.

"That is why I gave your name. You really care

for our people. I know that any decision you would make, it would be for the better of our race."

"Then why not make me your heir?" She gasped, shocked at the words that came out of her mouth. Her wolf stood with a howl that ricocheted through her.

What had she just said?

She couldn't believe that she had uttered those words.

"I never thought you would accept being my heir." Her grandfather appeared just as shocked as she was.

"I...I never thought about it before. It was always accepted that my father was your heir. But I —"

"Would be the better choice. You are intelligent, you give back to our people, and you never let your last name define who you were."

Ever since she was young, she had known she held no place in wolf shifter politics. Her parents ensured that she stayed in her place. She was to be the good little girl, get the best grades, wear pretty dresses, play an instrument, go to college, and get a job.

Never did they include her in anything the family represented.

They kept her separate and only brought her around when it was deemed appropriate or for them to look like the wholesome family.

She glanced up and found River's eyes on her from where she stood with Kira. River tilted her head as if to ask if she was okay. Kardia gave her a nod, knowing she was going to have to explain everything to her mate.

"So someone in our family had a magic wielder put a curse on me to try to prevent me from finding out about my seat on the second council. What do you think they are going to do if you make me your heir?"

"Our family wouldn't do this."

"Then who else would? Who is at risk to lose something if you change your heir? They knew what they were doing. How could I be your heir if I can't shift? I would never be accepted on any council."

"Then we will do what we must to break this curse."

"I can't be your heir." She closed her eyes. She felt a presence by her side and opened her eyes to find River standing next to her with a worried expression.

"What's wrong?" River whispered.

Kira sat on the ground in the middle of the yard, her lips moving in a silent chant.

"Everything is okay. I'll explain in a minute," she whispered to River.

Her mate jerked her head in a nod and jogged back over to join Kira. River sat next to Kira. Her wide eyes closed, and she chanted along with Kira.

She also needed to update her grandfather on what else had transpired since he had left Howling Valley.

"You cannot tell me what to do, young lady. But you are right about one thing. We must break this curse. If this is the work of your father and brother, then he will no longer be my heir."

"Papa—"

"He will be nothing to me." His sharp words sent a chill through her body. His voice had morphed into something fierce. "If he can do harm to his own child, then he won't think twice about making decisions that would harm our people. He can't be trusted."

"Papa, don't do anything crazy."

"I won't, but I will have my men look into this to get to the bottom of this. Whoever put this curse on you will pay," he growled. "And as for my son, he and I will have a little chat."

Kardia moved to the stairs on shaky legs and sat back down. She couldn't believe they were having this type of conversation. Even she was shocked at the revelation that all of this was probably because of her own flesh and blood.

She had always sensed that her father and brother were power hungry, but she didn't think they would ever go to this extreme to get what they wanted.

No wonder they had ignored her. Pushed her away.

They had assumed she was weak.

If she could fall under a magic wielder's spell and not shift, she couldn't honor the request of her grandfather to hold a seat on either of the councils.

How could they do this to her? What had she ever done to her family? Everything they wanted her to do, she did.

"We are waiting for another one of the witches from the coven to return. They think she will be able to lift the curse from me," Kardia said.

"Whatever the witch needs from me, you tell me, and it's yours," he said.

Wyett was in his councilman role. She could tell by his authoritative tone. It was cold and harder.

"We will break this curse," he said.

"Oh, and about the witch." She gave a dry chuckle. She might as well share everything with him at the moment. She didn't want to take any chances that something would happen to her and he would never know.

"What is it, my dear?"

"She's my mate."

CHAPTER TEN

Night had fallen, and the moon was high. River stared out the window of Kardia's home. She had sensed in a change in Kardia since she had spoken with her grandfather.

Kardia had caught River up on the phone call, but River sensed it bothered her. River couldn't fathom growing up in a household that didn't include love. Her heart ached for Kardia. River vowed in that moment that once this was all over, their home would be filled with love and happiness. Her mate would never feel unloved again.

She glanced over her shoulder and took in

Kardia sitting on the couch. Her feet were pulled underneath her as she stared off into nothing.

She hadn't really said much outside of sharing the discussion with her grandfather.

River blew out a deep breath and turned around. She leaned back against the windowsill and gazed at her mate.

"The ward is a strong one," River said, breaking the silence. Kira had left long ago after they had completed the spell to construct the magical fence that surrounded the property. "It should hold against anyone who tries to come here to do you harm."

Kardia nodded.

River flew across the room and sat next to Kardia. She pulled her into her arms, hugging her hard. Kardia held on to her tightly. River lost track of how long they sat like that. If this was what her mate needed, then she would stay for as long as Kardia needed her.

The energy that poured off Kardia was that of sadness, and it practically broke her heart.

"Are you hungry?" River asked. The day had been a long one, and they hadn't eaten since they'd left the diner.

"Not really," Kardia mumbled.

"You need to eat something. Let me see what you have in the kitchen and I'll make us some dinner." River sat back away from Kardia. She took her mate's face in her hands and plopped a big kiss on Kardia's lips. "Don't try to stop me. I'm here for you. You are mine and I'm yours, and I'm going to take care of you."

Kardia exhaled, a small smile appearing on her lips. Her facial features softened, and she visibly relaxed.

"Okay, River. Whatever you want to do."

River stood and went in the kitchen on a mission. She was determined to make them something good to eat. Her mate needed to keep her strength up.

Opening the fridge, she rummaged through it, pulling a few things out. She set her findings on the counter then moved over to the cabinets.

"What are you making?" Kardia leaned against the doorframe. Her amber eyes tracked River's every movement.

"Well, since you don't have any meat that isn't frozen, breakfast it is. I'll make us some pancakes."

"But I don't have pancake mix." Kardia frowned.

"Oh, posh! We don't do store-bought mix when

we can make it from scratch ourselves." River spun around with a smile on her lips. She held up the dry ingredients she'd need as if they were a prize.

"I'm impressed." Kardia sauntered into the kitchen and hopped up on the counter near the supplies.

"You're going to be full soon." River moved over to stand between Kardia's legs. She slid her hand along Kardia's thigh. Her mate's smooth brown skin felt wonderful under her fingertips.

Kardia leaned forward and met River for a breathtaking kiss.

Kardia's fingers threaded their way through River's hair, holding her tight. Their kiss deepened with their passion and lust for each other taking over. River brought Kardia to the edge of the counter, her hands on her ample bottom.

"You sure you want to cook right now?" Kardia asked. She rested her forehead on River's.

"Yes. You are not going to distract me with hot kisses." River giggled. She stepped back out of Kardia's embrace, immediately missing the feel of her. She tucked her thick hair behind her ear.

"Me, distracting? How can I concentrate when I can scent your arousal?" Kardia's amber eyes deepened as she watched River.

She squeezed her thighs together. How was she supposed to cook, knowing her mate could scent how wet she was for her?

"You can't tell me things like that." River barked a laugh. She took a bowl out of the cabinet and got to work constructing the pancake batter.

"I can't help it how good you smell." Kardia hopped down and came to stand behind River. She gently ran her fingers down River's spine, dropping a soft kiss on her shoulder.

A shiver rippled through River at the touch of her lover.

"It's growing stronger, and it just makes me want to lick you until you scream."

"Kardia." River whipped around to face her.

She reached up and pulled her wolf to her. Their kiss was frantic and desperate. River had every intention of making them something to eat, and she was going to do that. She pulled away before she stripped naked and allowed her mate to feast between her legs. "Grab a skillet for me, please?"

They were panting, and it was so hard to stop what they both wanted.

"The minute we are done eating, you will be

next on the menu for me." Kardia pressed a hard kiss to her lips and backed away.

River turned back to the bowl and tried to calm her body down. Her skin was practically on fire, and her panties were currently drenched. Now she had to focus.

What the hell was she supposed to be making?

Pancakes.

She had made them hundreds of times, and it was a chore to try to remember the recipe. Blowing out a deep breath, she got to it. They worked together in harmony, flirting and sharing kisses in between. But eventually, their meal was complete.

"Oh my. These are so good." River motioned to the big plate before her. She bit back a smile. For someone who had said she wasn't hungry, Kardia had loaded her plate up with five large flapjacks and was halfway through them.

"I'm glad you like them."

"No more pre-made stuff. I need to learn how to make them." Kardia smiled.

River's heart fluttered at the beauty of her mate. A good meal seemed to do the trick to bring Kardia back to her.

"Why do you need to make them? I can just make them whenever you want." River shrugged. It would be her pleasure to make them if they always brought a smile like this to Kardia's face.

"You would?" Kardia's expression reminded River of a kid being promised an endless supply of goodies. It just solidified that she was going to give Kardia whatever she wanted in life to make up for such a lonely upbringing. No longer was her mate going to feel alone or abandoned.

"Of course." River picked up her glass of milk and took a sip. "Anything for you, Kardia."

"You're going to spoil me." Kardia shook her head and went back to wolfing down her food.

River didn't hide her sneaky grin. Spoiling her was exactly what she had in mind.

"I know what I forgot." River pushed back from the table and went into the living room to snag her purse. When she and Kira were grabbing supplies for the ward at Rapture, she had purchased some-thing special for Kardia. She walked back into the room and went over to Kardia who was pushing her empty plate away.

There was a wolfish grin on her face as she watched River approach her.

"Want any more?" River asked.

"No, I'm good. I don't want to overdo it." Kardia patted her flat stomach.

River rolled her eyes. There was nothing wrong with her mate's figure. She was made perfect.

"What is that?" Kardia asked.

"This, my love, is an amulet I want you to wear." River held it up where they both could admire it. The necklace would provide another layer of protection for her mate. The rustic-bronze, ocular amulet held an amber jewel in the middle of it. It hung from a sturdy leather necklace. "It will protect you. Many call this an evil eye amulet. It will ward you against negative energy."

"Why do I need to wear an amulet, too?" Kardia asked.

River stood behind her and placed the necklace on her. She secured it before moving in front of Kardia. She leaned against the table and reached for the amulet.

"Because I can't expect you to stay on your property at all times. If you leave and go into town, this will protect you."

River closed her eyes, pushing a small sliver of her powers into it while she chanted a spell to enchant the amulet and activate its own powers.

Within this shield grant protection.
Divine goddess, hear my plea.
Protect my loved one.

Day or night.

I summon thee.

River opened her eyes, sensing the warmth from the amulet. As long as Kardia wore it, new negative energy shouldn't be able to affect her. It wouldn't be able to banish the curse from her, but it should keep her from coming under attack from any other magic wielder.

She released the amulet and placed it on Kardia's chest. Her gaze lifted and met Kardia's.

"Is everything good?" Kardia's voice was low and husky.

River bit her lip and nodded.

"Yeah. Always make sure you are wearing this when you leave home," River whispered.

Kardia's hands settled on her waist and guided her to stand between her legs. "I won't take it off. Ever."

River's breath caught in her throat as Kardia's hands slid up her thighs and rested on the waist of her shorts. She held River's gaze, her fingers quickly undoing the buttoned closure.

"What are you doing?" River asked.

Kardia's lips curved up in the corner, her hands continuing to work. The sound of the zipper cut through the air. River's heart pounded, the powerful rush of her desire surging through her. The knowing was flaring to life again. It was stronger than desire. A flood of emotions and need took over her.

She needed to bind herself to her wolf.

The universe was demanding it.

"I recall telling a certain witch that after I ate my dinner, she would be next."

River's shorts slid off to the floor. Her panties were next, landing on top of her shorts. Kardia didn't stop there. She tugged River's shirt over her head, dropping it on the growing pile of clothes. Her bra joined soon after.

Goosebumps littered her skin.

Kardia leaned forward and left a trail of kisses along her body. Her hands slid around to her plump bottom and cupped it.

River whimpered, basking in the sensation of Kardia pressing soft kisses to her stomach. She reached for her love, grasping her cheeks to tilt her face upward. River covered Kardia's lips with hers, kissing the woman she loved.

There was no doubt that she loved Kardia.

The knowing may have confirmed she was the one for her, but deep down, River had known the moment she'd met Kardia that she was special.

This woman needed her, and she would always be there for her to support her and love her.

Kardia stood from her chair and swept her arm across the table, pushing the dishes off onto the floor. They both ignored the sound of breaking crockery. Kardia lifted River by the back of her thighs and sat her on the table.

"I need you," Kardia whispered.

"I'm here. I'm not going anywhere." River closed the gap between them, silencing her lover with her mouth. She poured every ounce of love into the kiss.

Kardia returned the kiss with just as much passion.

Kardia broke it, trailing her mouth and tongue along River's jawline and down to her neck. River shivered at the sensation of Kardia's fangs scraping her sensitive skin. She tilted her head to give Kardia better access to her. Her core clenched at the thought of those sharp fangs sinking into her flesh.

Her desire poured from her center.

A gasp escaped her when Kardia nipped her. It wasn't enough to break the skin, but it certainly gave her the impression that her wolf was close to the surface, asserting her dominance over River.

River skated her fingers over Kardia's shoulders and went up to the base of her neck, diving into her soft dark hair.

"Hmmm…" River moaned.

Kardia's hands caressed her, molding to her mounds. River's head fell back. She moved her hands to brace herself on the table behind her. Kardia's lips captured River's nipple, suckling it into her warm mouth. Her free hand massaged and played with her other breast.

"Yes."

"I love your body," Kardia murmured.

Her tongue circled her beaded bud, gently biting down on it. The action sent a shock of electricity to River's core. Kardia straightened and pushed River down on the table.

"It's so beautiful. Perfect and all mine."

Her hands traced along River's twin mounds, trailing down her stomach. River's body writhed on the table. She spread her legs, her pussy aching for Kardia's attention. Her hips thrust upward, seeking either Kardia's hands or tongue.

Kardia's hand arrived at her waist. She dropped another kiss to her lower belly. A growl vibrated from Kardia. She placed her hands on

River's thighs, holding them open to present her pussy to her.

"Look at how wet you are for me," Kardia murmured. Her finger slid through River's folds, sinking inside her cunt.

River groaned, pushing her hips forward against Kardia's hand.

"Yes," she hissed.

"Mine." Kardia growled. She inserted another finger inside River, leaning down and capturing her clit with her mouth.

River cried out in joy. Her lover's tongue teased her swollen nub gently, suckling it with an increased pressure. Her fingers thrust in and out of River's drenched core. River reached out and gripped Kardia's hair. She thrust her hips against Kardia's mouth, wanting more.

"Yours," she whispered.

Kardia's eyes were closed as she feasted on River's pussy. Her body was Kardia's, and there wasn't anything she wouldn't let Kardia do to her. River's body trembled from the onslaught of emotions racing through her.

Kardia's fingers twisted inside her slick channel, pumping harder. She cried out, the pressure on her clit mounting. She tightened her fingers on Kardia's hair. She rode her lover's tongue until the breath was snatched from her from the orgasm commanding her body.

River arched off the table, a scream spilling from her lips. She fell back onto the table, panting. It took everything in her power not to bind herself to her wolf at this moment. She opened her eyes and took in Kardia lifting her head from between her legs. Kardia kissed her inner thigh. She withdrew her fingers from River, a smile appearing on her lips.

A whimper escaped River. Kardia's fingers stroked her clit, her smile growing wider. River's body refused to move. It was as if it wanted Kardia to have her way with her again.

"Best after-meal snack." Kardia pulled her chair up to the table and sat, her face level with River's core. "So tasty. I need more."

CHAPTER ELEVEN

River braced her hands on her hips, laughing at her students. The day was almost over, and the little ones were getting antsy in the classroom.

"Settle down," she said.

The laughter slowly faded as all the eyes settled on her. She walked over to her desk and rested back on it. She took in the wide eyes of all the children who would grow up to be talented witches and warlocks. The future of magic wielders was in her hands. Here in this classroom, she gave them a foundation to grow on.

Her heart leaped at the thought of her future

with Kardia. Maybe they could have a witch or wolf pups of their own. Kardia would make a great mother. She was fierce and protective. There was no doubt in River's mind that Kardia would be completely opposite to her parents and would love any and all of their offspring.

"Now, can anyone tell me why we would use protection spells?" River figured since she had recently cast one and enchanted Kardia's amulet, it would be best to speak about it with her class. Protection spells hadn't been on her lesson plan, but she wanted to slide it in for the time being.

A few of the students raised their hands. River was pleased to see that she had all of their attention.

"Connie, tell me why we would use a protection spell." River pointed to the blonde-haired student who was practically standing trying to get her attention.

"A protection spell will keep my bunny, Smurfette, safe from hawks," Connie replied with a straight face. She flopped down in her chair, her eyes growing wider. "My momma said we had to in order to keep the hawks from scooping her up and taking her away to another world."

She wasn't going to touch the "another world"

comment. She had no intention of bursting the kid's bubble that the hawk would be killing and eating Smurfette.

"Oh Goddess, yes." River held back her laugh. She remembered when she was a child she had placed a protection spell on her puppy, Waldo. He was known to wander away and get lost in the woods. For some magic wielder families, protection spells were taught early to keep the family pets safe. "What's another reason to use a protection spell?"

She pointed to another student.

"My mom said we had to protect our home to keep bad people away," Winter said. The pigtailed girl looked around the room at her fellow friends. "She said she hoped it kept that darn woman away from my daddy."

"Okay, yes. Protection spells." River spun around and moved over to her chalkboard. This conversation was getting interesting, and she wasn't sure the students' parents would appreciate family business being discussed in the classroom. River picked up a piece of chalk and wrote the word "protection" on the board. "For your homework, I want you to create a simple protection spell. It doesn't have to be a big one. Write it down and then bring it to class tomorrow."

Excitement spread through the room. The kids loved fun homework and always surprised her with their creativity. Constructing a spell from scratch would be a cool project for them.

The bell rang, and the kids jumped up from their chairs. They scrambled to gather their belongings. River tossed the chalk on her desk and moved over to the door that led outside. She pushed it open and took in the children already outside scurrying by. She turned and leaned against the door to allow her class to escape the building.

They poured out and joined in the melee.

"Slow down!" she shouted. Her gaze landed on a familiar figure making their way to her. River's smile widened. "What are you doing here?"

Kardia shrugged. A crooked grin appeared on her lips. River's hungry gaze took in her soul mate. She bit her lip, trying to hold back her reaction to Kardia. She didn't think becoming aroused in her classroom was professional.

"I was missing you, and I was in town, so I decided to come and surprise you." Kardia arrived at her side.

"Well, come on in and let me grab my things," River said.

She motioned for Kardia to follow her into the

classroom. She shut the door and moved over to her desk and gathered her belongings. Kardia ambled around the room, exploring. Her burned-orange dress stopped at her knees. A wide white belt encircled her waist, and matching sandals covered her feet. Her dark hair was left loose and rested on her shoulders

"Your kids are talented," Kardia said, pointing to the artwork posted on her far wall.

The one good thing about teaching magic in the local school, she got a chance to work with so many wonderful children each year. Her class was just like art, music, and gym. It was an extra class the students had the opportunity to take as an elective.

She got to work with all of the little magic wielders in the school and she loved it.

"That they are." Some of the kids wanted to display their work in her room to help decorate it, so she gave them a place to share their creations. "How was the job hunt?"

River tossed her bag on her shoulder and grabbed her keys. She was excited to hear about her day. Kardia was anxious to secure a job and find her place in Howling Valley. She had already buried her way into River's heart.

"It went great. I put in a few applications and I'm pretty sure I should get some calls."

They exited the room and walked through the building. Most of the teachers were racing out almost as fast as the students had. There were no meetings that required them to stay.

River waved to a few staff members as they navigated through the school. She just hoped no one would stop her. It was time to go home, and she wanted to snuggle up with Kardia. Since she and Kira had placed the protection ward on her property, everything had been silent. The hope was that everything would hold until they spoke with Cora—which it had. Today was the day they planned to go meet with Cora and Addy. The couple had invited them over for dinner.

Cora had to have an answer for them.

It she could break the curse, even better.

Kardia's wolf would be free, and they could claim each other and start their life together.

"Did you put in an application for Nightstar Inc.?" Nightstar Incorporated was a very renowned boating company own by the Gerwulfs. The company had been in the alpha's family for years. When the Gerwulf family settled in the Southern California town of Howling Valley, many of the first members of the Nightstar Pack were employed by the Gerwulfs.

The promise of steady employment, a beautiful, safe town to raise a family, and a fair alpha was too tempting to pass up. Their pack and town had grown, and the company became one of the most well-known boating companies in the world.

"No. I was too nervous to apply. The Gerwulfs have already done so much for me." Kardia took her hand, their fingers linking.

She gave a slight squeeze, and River's heart fluttered.

She was correct. Had it not been for the alpha recommending River to Kardia, they might have never met.

"That is true."

They left the school through a side door that led to the teacher parking lot. River guided them over to her car. There weren't too many vehicles left. River snorted. It would appear the teachers had wasted no time in leaving. Once they arrived at her car, she turned to Kardia.

"But you do know they would help you find a job."

"Jena was asking me about my job search the last time I met with them," Kardia said.

"See, she was probably waiting for you to apply." River bounced on the balls of her heels.

"But I was really hoping to get away from engineering and find something I'd be passionate about." Kardia released her hand and turned to face the playground located off in the distance. "I want to do something that gives my life a purpose. I want my life to mean something, help people."

River tossed her bag in the back seat of the car and slammed the door shut. She moved to stand behind Kardia. The frustration poured off the wolf in waves. River wrapped her arms around Kardia's waist, pulling her back to lean on her.

"It's okay. But don't count the Gerwulfs out entirely. If you don't want to stay in your field, I'm sure there is something else you can do."

Kardia leaned back with her hands covering River's. The hold felt so natural, as if they had been together for years. If she could, she would snap her fingers and take away all of Kardia's problems.

"I'm not. I'll keep them in the back of my mind." Kardia glanced over her shoulder with a sparkle in her amber eyes.

Her sexy grin sent River's heart racing.

Kardia spun around in River's arms. "Why

don't we go to your house so you can get ready for dinner."

"Where did you park your car?" River scanned the parking lot and didn't see it.

"On the street. There were so many cars with the kids getting out, I just parked down there and walked."

"I'll take you to your car and we can head to my house."

"Sounds like a plan." River stole a quick kiss before backing away.

CHAPTER TWELVE

Kardia stepped from River's car and shut the door. She waved and walked to hers. She was excited about the day. She had some leads on jobs, and the urge to see River had been strong. Her animal was demanding to see her, and they were close by, so she had made her way to the school. Unfortunately, she was arriving at the time the parents were lining up to wait for their children to run from the school so she had to park a ways away.

She hadn't minded the walk. It was a beautiful day, and the sun was shining. Kardia gave a mother wave and spun back to her car. The sound of her phone ringing came from inside her bag. Kardia frowned, recognizing the ringtone. She dug in her shoulder bag to find it.

"What's wrong?" River called out.

"My phone is ringing. It's my father. I should probably take this." Kardia took her phone out and slid her fingertip across the screen.

River moved her car and pulled in front of Kardia's to free up the street.

"Hello?" Kardia opened her car and got into the driver's seat. It had been months since she'd spoken with her father. She wasn't sure what he could possibly want from her.

"Well, hello, my dear," her father's voice boomed.

She pressed the start button and turned her car on. Hopefully, this call wouldn't take long.

"It's been a long time since we've spoken," he said.

"I know. I've been a little busy."

"I had heard you had moved to some small town. Hawking Valley?"

"No, Howling Valley." Had her grandfather shared this information with him? She hadn't wanted to tell her father anything about where she was. Not that he would pay much attention to her.

She could tell him everything, and it wouldn't mean anything. It didn't have anything to do with their family and something he could spotlight.

"Who told you that?"

"I sent Tomas to your house, and imagine my surprise when I find out my daughter had moved and hadn't told anyone."

Tomas was one of her father's wolves who worked for him. He was a shady character who made her uncomfortable by just being in the same room. He didn't speak much, but he was completely loyal to her father.

"What did you want?"

"I can't check up on my daughter?"

Kardia snorted. If her father wanted to truly check up on her, he could have come himself, but he hadn't. He'd sent the help.

"Papa knew," she murmured.

"Oh, I'm sure he did. The two of you are thick as thieves. Always scheming together."

She wasn't going to give in to him. Her father was searching for something. She wondered if her grandfather had called him. This was just too coincidental that he'd decided to call her today.

"So when were you going to call me and your mother and tell us you'd moved?"

"I don't know. I'm still getting settled and looking for a job," she replied nonchalantly. Her gaze landed on River's car, and she needed to get him off the phone so she and her mate could go about their day.

"How are you doing?"

Kardia rolled her eyes and bit back a sigh. She knew exactly what he wanted to know. He was asking if she was still unable to shift. Well, she wasn't going to tell him anything she had learned. If what she thought was true, then she didn't want to alert him that she was onto him and whoever he may have had curse her.

"I'm doing good."

There, short and sweet.

"How are you really doing?" he snapped.

She smiled, sensing his exacerbation through the phone. Her father did not have patience, and it was a wonder for someone who would be on the council one day, she would think that person would need the patience of a saint.

"I'm fine."

She blinked, a weird sensation overcoming her. She frowned, not sure what this was. She blinked, her vision becoming cloudy. She swallowed, sitting forward. An ache blossomed in her chest. It almost felt as if an elephant was sitting on top of her. She fell back, gasping for breath.

What the hell was going on?

The phone fell from her hand. She gripped the steering wheel and fought to drag air into her lungs. Her wolf howled, desperately urging her to move and get out of the car. She reached for the handle, but she couldn't get her hand to release the steering wheel.

Kardia closed her eyes and tried not to panic, but it was overtaking her. She didn't know what this was, but she fell into a quiet darkness.

K ardia inhaled sharply, a fiery pain ripping through her chest. A groan slipped from her lips as she rolled over. Whatever she was lying on was hard and unforgiving. The scent of nature assaulted her senses.

Her eyes flew open, and she froze in place.

Where the hell was she?

She blinked again, unable to believe what she was seeing. No longer was she in her car. Her heart slammed against her chest, and she found herself lying on the ground in a wooded area.

The sky was painted black with a few winking stars.

Goosebumps spread along her arms. She pushed up off the ground and stood. Her hands had dirt and leaves on them. She brushed them off on her pants and froze. Even her clothes were different. She was dressed in leggings, a t-shirt, and tennis shoes.

Kardia took a step and stumbled, almost falling back down. She felt as weak as a brand-new pup who was walking for the first time. She righted herself and spun around.

"No," she whispered. The area was eerily familiar to her. The tall trees, the thick brush, and a pathway that led into the spooky woods.

She had been here before.

There was no way she was where she thought she was.

No, she refused to believe it.

How could she be back in the same woods where her attack had happened? The hairs on her arms stood up at attention. This was her nightmare coming true. There was no way she'd transported here.

She was sitting in her car, with her mate in the car in front of her. This had to be a dream. But how did she fall asleep? She had been on the telephone with her father.

Kardia pinched herself and yelped.

She was very much awake here.

"How can this be?" she whispered. Her gaze moved to the path, not seeing anything. She glanced over her shoulder, and only now, there was no mountain cliff. Only another thicket of woods. This, at least, was different than before when she'd been attacked. Kardia scanned the area and didn't see anything.

You can't stay. Move, her wolf warned.

Kardia gulped, unsure in which direction to go. Did she want to go down the scary-looking path?

"This would be the time I'd need you now," she murmured to her animal. Her wolf had always been brave, ferocious, and protective of her. Her wolf wouldn't have hesitated running off down the long path into the unknown.

No answer from her wolf.

"Of course." She sighed. The sounds of nature would have been comforting had this been a place she wanted to be. A few calls of the wild were unsettling. She jumped at a screeching sound that came from somewhere behind her. "Looks like forward we are going."

Inhaling sharply, she made her decision. Off she'd go down the long, dark pathway. Her feet carried her along the dirt. She didn't know where it would lead, but she followed the path. Something was pushing her farther into the woods.

"There are no shadow monsters," she whispered. Hopefully, speaking her wish out loud would keep all creatures away, but the uneasy feeling in the pit of her stomach was a warning. The path grew even more narrowed. The woods thickened; the moonlight barely broke through the treetops. Thank goodness for her shifter vision that allowed her to see.

The uneasy feeling was growing. Kardia suspected she wasn't alone. Her ears strained to pick up any noises behind her. Whoever or whatever was stalking her was completely silent. Kardia's first instinct was to run, but in her human form, she would have a hard time outrunning any beast.

Kardia paused and glanced over her shoulder. The trail she had just taken was barely visible. She stared in disbelief. How had the landscape changed?

"What in the—?"

She was cut off by a low growl echoing off in

the distance. She walked backward, squinting to see. The pit of her stomach gave way watching the black misty cloud drifting from the trees. Kardia's eyes widened.

Not again.

She shook her head and took steps backward. This couldn't be happening to her again. The shadowy figure swirled around in the air and took the figure of a wolf, growing to triple her size. Its growl menacing and threatening. It grew louder, sending a spike of fear through her. She quickened her pace, not taking her eyes off the figure.

It advanced on her, and there was nothing else she could possibly do but run. Kardia spun on her heels and took off down the trail. She urged herself as fast as she could go, but it wasn't enough. The shadowy mist swirled around her. A screamed escaped her as the wolf's dark mist surrounded her.

Kardia's feet were swept from underneath her. She fell to the ground with a cry. Once again, she was racked with the piercing pain of fangs and claws sinking into her body. She kicked and swung her arms, trying to fight off her assailant.

She refused to go out without a fight. She had so much to live for. Tears streamed down her face at the thought of never seeing River again. How could fate be so cruel to bring her mate to her but not allow her to claim her? Spend the rest of her life with her?

Why?

"Leave me alone!" she screamed.

Her fists cut through the air but failed to land on her attacker. Her skin grew slick with the blood the wolf drew out. She rolled over onto her hands and knees to push up off the ground. It was obvious she wasn't going to be able to defend herself from this entity.

Kardia stumbled to her feet and made an attempt to run, but the mist encircled her. She screamed, swinging her arms to defend herself. She rushed forward, her adrenaline giving her the strength she needed. The path before her was free and clear. She took off down the trail, the howl of the wolf behind her.

Her arms pumped while she ran. The trail grew darker, the thick brush not allowing the moon's rays to pierce through the thick treetops. Her wolf's senses enhanced, allowing her to scent and hear everything around her. Ignoring the pain and warm trails of blood sliding down her arms and legs, she kept going.

Crashing sounded behind her. It was gaining on

her. She dared not turn around to look. She didn't know where she was going, she only knew she had to get away from that monster. She came to a fork in the trail, and she didn't have a clue which way to go. She skidded to a halt momentarily.

Right or left.

"Fuck," she muttered.

Kardia could feel the heat of the wolf behind her. She took the left path and prayed she wasn't running into her death. The snarls and growls were right behind her. She cried out as something slammed into her. She went flying down on the ground.

Her scream escaped her. Fangs sank into her shoulder and tossed her body through the air. She crashed into a tree, crumpling to the ground. She rolled over onto her side, barely able to move from the pain. She whimpered and lifted her head. The ghostly figure of the wolf prowled to her. She blinked to clear her vision. Warm rivers of a thick liquid trailed down her forehead and balanced on her eyelashes. She inhaled, scenting her blood.

This was it.

The curse that was cast upon her was going to end her life.

An image of River came to her mind.

Her love.

The one for her.

Kardia braced herself. There was no more running. If she was going to die, then she'd go out at least standing.

She used what energy she had left and pushed up and got to her feet. Her muscles screamed in protest. Her shoulder felt raw, while her body ached in ways she'd never experienced before. She inhaled sharply and regretted it.

Kardia stood to her full height and glared at the beast.

"You want me, come and get me."

CHAPTER THIRTEEN

"Tell me everything."

River glanced up at Cora and nodded. Tears slid down her cheeks as she stared down at Kardia. River had never felt the fear that she had experienced when she had first arrived at the door of Kardia's car. She had never seen something like this.

River had been sitting in her car waiting for Kardia to signal she was done with her phone call. After about fifteen minutes, River sensed something was wrong. She had peeked in her rearview mirror and hadn't seen Kardia moving. River had got out of her vehicle and walked to Kardia's. What she saw had her screaming.

Her mate was sitting in her car, as if frozen.

"She didn't respond to me at all. No matter how many times I called her name, she didn't even move." River's voice broke. More tears flowed down her cheeks while she watched her mate. She reached up and wiped her face with the back of her hand.

A couple of homeowners who had been chatting with each other had heard her scream. They had raced over to help her. Every moment after that was a blur. Somehow, they had put Kardia in the back of River's car so she could go get help.

The only place she could think of was to go to the White Lotus. Her coven would help them. Somehow in the rush, she had even called Cora who'd immediately agreed to meet them at their sanctuary.

River sighed, feelings of sorrow overtaking her. What was happening to her mate? How could she not help her?

They were currently located in the healing room. It was a room that drew power from the moon. The ceiling had a retracting glass shield that allowed the moon and sun to shine down in the center. Her mate lay stretched out on the floor where they normally held their prayers and rituals.

River's gaze landed on Kardia's neck. She froze in place. She reached up and pulled the neck of her shirt down and didn't see the amulet she had given Kardia. Where was it? River looked around but didn't see it anywhere. Her heart pounded. That was how the magic wielder had been able to get their hands on her mate. She didn't have her protective ward on her to keep evil away from her.

"This is definitely the work of dark magic," Cora murmured. Her dark hair flowed around her shoulders as she leaned over Kardia with her palm hovering above her forehead.

"That's why I thought it best to bring you in to help us," River said. She unconsciously reached for Kardia's limp hand. She brought it to her lips and pressed a kiss to the back of it. Kardia's body was so still. If it wasn't for the slight rise and fall of her chest, River would be worried. "She's been suffering from this for so long."

"We will find a way to help your mate." Cora offered her an understanding smile.

River knew the story of Cora and Addy. They'd had trials and tribulations when they'd first found each other. Cora's old coven leader had it out for her bad. It was no wonder Cora didn't trust covens after her last one. Thankfully, the strong witch decided to stay in Howling Valley and join the White Lotus.

"If there is one thing I hate, it's dark magic and attacking the innocent," Cora said.

"Thank you." Relief spread through River. Knowing Cora wasn't going to stop until she'd helped them was comforting.

"What is going on in here?" a familiar voice asked from the doorway.

River turned and took in her grandmother, Jimma, and her mother, Celeste. The mother-and-daughter duo were similar in build and had almost identical facial features. Only Jimma had more gray hair than her daughter.

"And is that the wolf Evan Gerwulf wanted you to help?"

River nodded, unable to speak. She feared if she did, the waterworks would start. Her mother and grandmother flew into the room. They knelt by Kardia's body.

"She is under the control of a dark witch. Someone who means to do her harm," Cora announced.

River whimpered at Cora's words. She knew

her friend didn't mean anything by it, but just hearing that someone wanted to harm Kardia was like taking a sword to the heart. The piercing pain was just unbearable. She rocked back and forth and held on to Kardia's hand. She wanted her mate to be able to feel her. No matter where she was mentally, River wanted her to know that she was there with her. She didn't want her wolf to ever feel alone and lonely again.

"Who is this woman to you?" Celeste asked. She laid a warm hand on River's shoulder.

River didn't have to look to know that all eyes were on her. She wasn't ashamed to admit anything. She was actually proud and happy that she would be able to tell her mother and grand-mother at the same time. River had a sense that Cora had already figured out the relationship between her and Kardia.

"This is Kardia Markway, and she is my soul mate. The knowing inside me awakened the very moment we met." Her lips curled into a small smile thinking of the moment she'd first laid eyes on Kardia.

"Oh, River. That is wonderful." Her mother gave her shoulder a squeeze.

"I knew something beautiful was going to come

out of you two meeting." There was a twinkle in her grandmother's eyes.

River chuckled. Of course her grandmother would know something would come out of the two of them meeting. She always had a sixth sense about people.

"Now we will have plenty of time to catch up," her grandmother said. "Someone tell us what is going on."

Cora glanced over at her as if waiting for permission to fill them in. River nodded, unable to go through the story again. Just the memories alone were enough to give her nightmares for a long time. She closed her eyes to try to block out some of the story. Instead, she focused on her mate. She gripped Kardia's hand harder and tried to push some of her healing powers into her.

What good was having the ability to help heal if she couldn't even help the one woman she loved?

River paused at the revelation. She wasn't surprised that she had fallen in love with Kardia. The goddess had gifted her the most enchanting woman to love and cherish. Kardia was a woman who deserved someone to shower her with love for all eternity. River believed her mate would awaken so she could do just that.

River concentrated harder and sent a wave of energy into Kardia. She sensed a connection with her. Maybe if she could tap into her subconscious, she could reach Kardia's wolf like she had before. It could give her a chance to figure out what was going on. River pushed harder, trying to reach out to Kardia, but she slammed against a dark wall.

She jerked back, surprised at Kardia's body twitching in response. Her jerk cut Cora off from the story.

"What's wrong with her?" Jimma asked.

Kardia thrashed on the floor as if fighting off an attacker. Her movements grew wilder, and River's hand slipped from Kardia's.

"I don't know. I was trying to reach her, and it was as if someone has constructed a barrier between us." River fought back tears watching her loved one writhe around.

"Whoever put this curse on her doesn't want her saved." Cora met River's gaze with a grim one of her own. "Let me see if I can try to break through. She's going to need our help, and if I can get in, maybe I can get a reading of who is controlling her subconscious."

"Will it hurt her?" River bit her lip. Whatever Kardia was battling against was hurting her.

Blood seeped from Kardia's nose. It slowly ran down the side of her face, leaving a trail of redness against her brown skin.

"I'll be as gentle as I can," Cora replied.

River hesitated. Her mate had been through so much and was apparently fighting for her life. River had never felt so helpless before. Tears poured down her face.

"We have to trust Cora," Celeste murmured softly. She placed a hand on River's shoulder. Her mother's warm embrace surrounded her. She pressed a soft kiss to River's head.

River welcomed her mother's hug and strength.

"Do it." River nodded. She had faith in Cora. It was this invisible enemy she didn't trust. Kardia had agreed to let Cora help her. Now was the time she would need a witch as powerful as Cora.

Cora laid a hand on Kardia's forehead. The whites of Cora's eyes appeared. Kardia's body continued to writhe. Sweat appeared on the wolf's skin. She was being mentally tortured.

"Open the skylight to let in the moon's rays," Jimma ordered.

Celeste jumped up and raced across the room to the panel on the wall. River hopped up and went over to one of the supply cabinets and grabbed some towels. She turned. Her grandmother grabbed a few herbs from the supply cabinet. Her mother joined Jimma, their conversation low. River ignored them, gathering what she needed for Kardia.

River had to do something to keep busy while Cora tried to help Kardia. She returned to Kardia and Cora. The rays of the moon shined down on them while the dark, cloudless sky showcased the large, round moon. Its power would assist Cora. She, like all witches, would draw from the power that was the moon.

Whatever Cora was doing must be working. Kardia wasn't struggling as hard. Her motions slowed down to small, inconsistent movements. River knelt next to her head and used the towels to wipe the sweat from her face as best she could while Cora's hand remained on her forehead. She dabbed at the blood still seeping from her nose. It tore her apart that her mate was suffering.

"Here, River. Drink this." Jimma knelt by River with a mug in her hand. Steam drifted from it along with a tantalizing aroma.

River dropped the towels next to her and took the mug from her.

"Thank you," she whispered.

"You will need to keep your strength up for her. Your mother went to grab us food and to alert the coven that we are in need of prayers."

River took a sip of the tea, and she smiled.

Dandelion tea.

It was made perfectly. The strong brew would help get the dark thoughts and negative energy away.

Kardia's body finally grew still.

River lost track of how much time had passed. She hadn't eaten much of the food her mother had brought her. Worry had taken over her, and it didn't leave much of an appetite for her.

Cora, on the other hand, was relentless. She had yet to break her connection with Kardia. She had been at this for hours.

River wished she could see what her friend was seeing. She was sure whatever or whoever Cora was going up against, she would be the victor. It was unbelievable what this witch could do. Her powers were unmatched by anyone River had ever known. When Cora had first arrived in town, she had constructed an entire ward around Howling Valley. The amount of power it took to do that and the fact she had continued to live her life while doing it was a testament to her strength.

River remembered it as if it were yesterday. The coven had grown weary, not knowing who was putting the magical barrier around their town. They hadn't known at the time whether it was a friendly or an enemy entrapping their powers. Imagine their surprise when it was revealed that it was an Omer woman.

Only one with power no one had ever seen before.

River handed her empty mug to her mother who swept away. River turned her attention back to Kardia and Cora. The two were silent and still. Cora's dark hair flowed around her shoulders from the breeze that floated through the massive skylight. Their coven had arrived. The women and men of the White Lotus were outside chanting and lending their power.

A whimper escaped Kardia. River sat forward on her knees, anxious to see if she would awaken. Cora grunted, a glow illuminating from her hands.

"Oh no," River murmured, sensing something was going wrong.

Cora frowned while Kardia's body arched from the floor.

"Ah!" Cora flew back and fell backward onto the floor. Kardia's body trembled and twitched.

"What is wrong?" River cried out.

The air around them grew warm, and the shimmer of magic surrounded them. Within moments, she watched Kardia's body shift. White fur sprouted out and spread along her brown skin, while her bones lengthened and reshaped. Her clothing shredded, not withstanding the growth in size and the reconfiguration of its owner.

Finally, a white wolf lay before them.

"Kardia?" River reached for her, her fingers diving in the soft fur.

The wolf's eyes remained closed, her breathing steady and slow. This was Kardia's wolf. She appeared the same as the vision River had been able to access.

"Wake up, my love. It is I, River."

River hiccupped, unable to stop the flow of tears. Her mate had waited for so long to be able to change into her animal. Now that she had, would she wake up?

Was her nightmare over?

"I know who is behind this," Cora announced. She crawled back over to Kardia, her gaze frantically scanning Kardia. "A powerful warlock who does this kind of thing for fun and coin. I should have known the moment you told me what was happening to her, what you've seen."

"Why isn't she waking up?" River's body shook as she was racked with tears. She leaned her forehead down onto Kardia's head, praying to the goddess above.

"She's imprisoned. I've seen her. I tried to help her, but he found me." Cora's voice was grim. Her warm hand came to rest on River's.

"How will we get her out? If her body is here?" River lifted her head and took in the firm look on Cora's face. The witch was pissed off.

How could she free her mate's mind?

"There is a way. You and I can go in to the Realm of Shadows. It will be tricky, but I'm sure I can do it."

River glanced down at her white wolf and knew without a doubt that she would try any and everything to free her mate. She would not let Kardia down. She didn't even have to ask what would be needed of her.

The Realm of Shadows didn't sound like a walk in the park. The name alone sent a chill of trepidation through her. She had to be strong for her mate. River couldn't be like everyone else in Kardia's life who pushed her to the side and ignored her. This was her mate. The one she was to bind her life to for all eternity.

She couldn't give up on her. River inhaled sharply, and a sense of calmness overtook her. She would have to be brave for Kardia. Put aside all fear of the unknown.

She nodded to Cora.

River would do and give anything to free her mate.

CHAPTER FOURTEEN

Kardia wrapped her arms around her knees, huddled in the corner of the cave she had been thrown in. Her body ached in ways that were impossible for any human being to withstand. Being a shifter, she had the ability to heal fast. Here, her wounds weren't healing as quickly as they would if she were able to shift. She glanced down at the slashes, cuts, and bruises that lined her arms and legs. Her shoulder wound was the worst. The wolf's fangs had sunk deep into her. Her muscles were stiff and tight. She could barely move it.

Kardia grimaced at the pulsating pain that was now dull and was a gentle reminder that it was still there.

She scanned the dark shadows of her surroundings. The hairs on her arms stood at attention. She didn't know how long she had been there. The cave was cold and damp. From the little she could see of it, she was the only being there.

She had suffered at the hands of the shadowy wolf until a cloaked man had come. Kardia hadn't seen his face, only his pale hands with long fingers. She had caught sight of his darkened fingertips; the nails were as black as the night sky. Without even touching her, he'd used his magic to drag her behind him.

No matter how much she'd fought against the invisible restraints that held her, she was unable to free herself. Up the mountain they had gone until they'd come to a series of caves that were tunneled through the earth. Her throat was still raw from her screaming and yelling, demanding he release her. By the time they'd arrived at what would be her cave, she'd been pleading for her life.

Pleading to be released.

But his only response had been a deep cackle of a laugh.

Kardia had tried to leave the cave. There was nothing she could see preventing her. It wasn't until she'd slammed into an invisible forcefield that she'd realized he had used magic to prevent her escape. So she'd hidden in the farthest corner of the dwelling, awaiting her demise.

It wasn't until she'd seen the witch that she'd felt an inkling of hope. It was the witch, Cora, the one who River had wanted her to go to for help. Cora, her dark hair flowing around her as she had walked up to the mouth of the cave. There was a shimmering light surrounding her.

"Kardia," Cora whispered fiercely.

Kardia pushed up off the ground where she had been lying. It was hard and unforgiving, but at the moment it was all she had. Her body screamed in protest when she stood, her gaze locked on the ethereal-looking woman. All of her instincts told her she could trust this woman, but she didn't want to be too sure.

"Who are you?" Kardia asked. She was hesitant to go near the entrance. She didn't know what the cloaked man wanted with her or who'd put him up to it.

"I'm Cora. A friend of your mate."

"Where is River? Is she okay?" Kardia limped over to Cora. From her recent experience with the invisible wall, she kept her distance from it.

"*She is fine. She is currently by your body——*"

"*My body?*" Kardia gasped in disbelief. She glanced down at herself and held her hands out. If this wasn't her body, then where the hell was she? How was she here?

"*Yes. I don't have much time to explain. This is the Realm of Shadows, and a powerful magic wielder has you trapped here. Have you seen who did this to you?*"

"*There was the cloud mist that was in the shape of a wolf,*" she murmured. Kardia glanced at her surroundings with a new set of eyes. Was any of this real?

"*It is real,*" Cora stated.

Kardia's head flew in her direction. Had the witch read her mind?

"*And no, I can't read minds. I'm very good at reading expressions. As I said before, we don't have much time. Did you see who entrapped you here?*"

Kardia swallowed hard.

"*Not really. There was a cloaked figure who brought me up here. I couldn't see his face.*" Panic settled in Kardia. Would this person keep her here for eternity? Her mind and body couldn't survive being separated. She may not know magic or witchcraft, but she understood that much. "*But I saw his hands. They were very pale, but the tips of his fingers were black, as were his nails.*"

"*Dashiel Maganti,*" Cora breathed.

"You know him? Can you save me?" Kardia took a step toward Cora. Hope blossomed in her chest. River had said that Cora was one of the most powerful witches around. Just by her being here and finding her proved that Cora was working with extreme power. If her mate trusted this witch, then Kardia would also.

"I believe I can." Cora's gaze roamed Kardia. Her eyes narrowed on her, a curse releasing from her lips. *"You are injured and in pain. Come closer."*

"I can't come too close. There is an invisible wall here." Kardia raised her good arm to gesture to the transparent field.

"Be still. I can take some of your pain away." Cora gave a nod, lifting a hand toward Kardia.

A white light shone bright from her hands. Kardia immediately felt a warmth overtake her. The energy pushed away the pain that had racked her body. She could feel the muscles and tendons healing. She stood, accepting the regenerating powers that flowed through her.

A gasp escaped her. Kardia rotated her injured shoulder, no longer feeling pain. She felt brand-new. She opened her eyes and watched Cora fling her arms away from her, sending whatever she pulled from Kardia away into the atmosphere.

"Thank you," Kardia murmured. She felt more relaxed than she had since arriving in this realm. She glanced down at her arms, and no longer were they marred by wounds and

blood. Her skin was once again restored. "How will you get me out of here?"

"First, let's see if I can just open the door." Cora motioned to the invisible divider between them. She stepped closer as if to study it. Satisfied with whatever she saw, she stepped away. "Move. I'm going to see if I can break through this and release you. Then we will return you to your body."

Kardia moved away, anxious to be free. She didn't want to see this Dashiel Maganti again. She just wanted to go home with River.

Her wolf paced at the thought of their mate.

They had to get back to her.

They would claim her.

Even if she would never shift again, she'd be okay with it. All she ever needed in this world was River.

She was all that mattered.

Kardia watched Cora's light grow brighter, illuminating the area around her. She rested her hands on the ward and grimaced. Her powers rushed forward, revealing the invisible shield that blocked Kardia's escape.

Kardia bit back a gasp watching the shield develop cracks in it. Her heart raced as she waited for it to shatter. She braced herself, ready to rush through the opening the minute it broke.

A dark-blue electricity bolt crashed into Cora. She flew

in reverse, away from the shield. The cracks slowly receded. It became whole again before disappearing from sight.

"No!" Kardia raced forward, crashing into the ward. She banged on it, trying to break free.

Cora's body lay on the ground. She rolled over and stood to her feet, facing someone out of Kardia's eyesight.

"Let her go, Dashiel," Cora demanded.

"You may be powerful, Cora Latimer, but you don't rule this realm," a deep baritone voice boomed. Out of the shadows, the cloaked figure appeared.

This was Dashiel, the warlock who had imprisoned her. Anger filled Kardia at the thought of this warlock ensnaring her. Who'd paid him? A growl escaped her; she watched him square off with Cora.

"And you have no right to trap an innocent." Cora's hands illuminated. The air around her whipped her hair around. If this wasn't a life-or-death situation, Kardia would be in awe of the witch. Her powers and strength radiated enough where even Kardia could feel it.

"Innocent? There are no innocents when it comes to war."

"The wolves' wars don't involve us, Dashiel. Or have you stooped low enough to be a paid warlock, only wanting the coins? I didn't think even the black magic wielders were low enough to take bribes."

"Bribes? How about getting paid by those who would have used my services anyway? Why shouldn't I be paid?" His laugh sent a chill through Kardia. If more dark witches and warlocks easily sold out their services, it could lead to a catastrophe.

Wolves' war?

Who was at war, and why was this the first time she'd heard of this?

"You will free her, Dashiel."

"And if I don't?"

"Do you want to really test me? I'm not the young girl I used to be," Cora warned.

Kardia didn't know what that meant, but even she didn't want to see all that Cora could do. The witch's light grew brighter, casting them all in her energy.

"Oh, I think I do want to test you." A dark energy rolled in, slamming into Cora's light.

Kardia instinctively moved back. With two magic wielders battling in front of her, there were bound to be casualties. Dashiel's darkness surrounded Cora.

Kardia's wolf stopped her pacing. She crashed against Kardia's stomach. Kardia almost fell back from the force of her animal.

Let me out, *her wolf demanded.*

Tears clouded Kardia's vision. It was the first time in ten years her wolf wanted to be released.

We are trapped, *she reminded her animal.*

She needs our help, *her beast growled.*

Fine. *Kardia was going to trust her. It had been too long since she had turned over the reins to her wolf, and if she thought she was the better one to help Cora, then she'd let her out.*

Kardia cried out as her beast pushed forward. Her white fur spread over her skin. She welcomed the pain from the change. She felt like a new pup shifting for the first time.

Cora shrieked, but Kardia was unable to look at her. The shift was consuming her as her body began the change. Her bones stretched and molded. Her fangs broke free from her gums.

"Oh, I don't think so," Dashiel hollered.

Kardia screamed, and a massive amount of energy burst through her. Pain lanced through her middle, seeming to set her on fire. It felt as if her body was splitting in two. Kardia fell to the ground, her body writhing from this new torture. She'd never felt anything like this. Her wolf's howl echoed in her head, growing farther away.

Kardia reached for her animal as if she could grab her. She felt the distance growing between them. In her mind, she saw her wolf clawing for her.

They were being ripped apart from each other.

"No!" *Kardia hollered, feeling her wolf slip away from her. She was left with a hollow space in her chest. She rolled* over onto her stomach, tears streaming down her face. She glanced up, only to see Dashiel standing at the entrance. His hood kept his features hidden.

There was no sight of Cora.

"They think they can rescue you? But I assure you, they cannot. That girl thinks she is more powerful than me? She has another think coming. There is no beating dark magic."

He entered the cave, stopping inches from her. Kardia crawled away from him, until her back hit a sharp wall. She didn't take her eyes off him, not trusting what he would do. She searched inside herself, trying to feel an inkling of her wolf, but it was silent. Had he really separated them? How was this even possible?

"Who is paying you?" Kardia whispered. Her arms came to wrap around herself. It was the only piece of comfort she had at the moment.

"Wouldn't you like to know, but know they are powerful and don't take too kindly to wolves with too much power." He spun around and walked out of the cave. He paused, looking at her over his shoulder. "I'm sure this will all be over now. Once I prove to them that I have your mind here, they will give me my money. As for your body, I'm sure you're smart enough to know the mind and body cannot live without one another."

Kardia shivered and watched him walk away. She blinked back tears of sorrow. She had once thought herself *to be alone before, but now, she was even more so. She had never been without her beast. She was a shell of her former self. Her wolf was gone, her body separated from her mind. If Cora was unable to save her, what hope did she have?*

Kardia blinked back the memories of the events leading up to now. The wounds that had been healed by Cora were back. It was strange what happened once her wolf had been taken away. It was as if she were human. All of the aches and pains had returned. For a brief moment, she had been healed, felt stronger, and had hope that she would escape.

But Dashiel had snuffed it all out.

Now she waited in this cave, preparing to die. Had she dreamed it all? Had Cora really come? She tried to reach out for her animal and was met with quietness.

"River," she whispered. She leaned her head back against the rocks, feeling not only the emptiness she was left with, but heartache as well. "I love you."

She closed her eyes, basking in the warm tears that slid down her cheeks. Her mate would never know she loved her. She hadn't said the words out loud, but she had tried to show her. She had thought they could save those sacred words for when they claimed each other.

They shouldn't have delayed sharing their true feelings.

Now, she may never get to say those three magic words.

CHAPTER FIFTEEN

River stood in the corner of the room, watching the councilman sit on the bed next to his grand-daughter. River knew how much Kardia loved her grandfather. The white wolf had yet to open her eyes. She hadn't been sure how to get a hold of him, so they had contacted Evan to update him on the situation. He and his wolves had immediately come and taken Kardia.

River refused to leave her side. She held out hope that she would awaken. They were in the infirmary located on the wolf pack's land. Their healers had no answers for the sudden change besides the retelling of the story Cora had shared with them all.

"How long has she been in her wolf form?" Markway asked.

"It's been two days, sir," River cleared her throat and answered. It had been the longest two days of her life. When Cora claimed there was a way they could enter the Realm of Shadows, she had been immediately ready, but they would have to wait. They needed the full moon in order to do that.

Thankfully, tonight was the full moon.

Together, she and Cora would venture into the other realm and rescue her mate.

"We are doing everything that we can to help her," Evan stated from the doorway.

"I'm sure you are. I just can't stand to see my granddaughter like this. It's been so long since she'd shifted, I had almost forgotten how beautiful her animal is." The older man stroked Kardia's fur. He blew out a sigh and turned to look at River. It was the first time he'd really noticed her since entering the room. His attention had been on Kardia the moment he'd stepped foot in the infirmary. There was a striking resemblance between the two of them. Their skin tone was the same russet brown, and their almond-shaped eyes were almost identical. "And you must be River, my granddaughter's mate."

"She told you?" River's eyebrows shot up high. She hadn't known Kardia had shared their relationship with her grandfather.

"Of course she did. Finding one's mate isn't something to hide away." He chuckled softly. His gaze went back to Kardia. "I'm glad you found each other. My granddaughter deserves the best in life."

"That I can agree." River nodded. She moved closer to the infirmary bed and knelt beside it.

"Who would do such a thing to her?" Markway rested his hand on Kardia's paw. His voice deepened, his amber eyes glowing.

"The witch who was able to make contact with Kardia is here." Evan moved aside to allow Cora to come through.

She had left, needing to do some research. She had promised River she would return. They all turned their attention to her as she walked to the foot of the bed.

"Greetings, sir." Cora nodded to Markway.

"You know who has done this to my granddaughter?" Markway's hand tightened on Kardia's paw.

"Yes, sir. A warlock by the name of Dashiel Maganti is keeping her hostage in the Realm of Shadows, sir. From what I was able to gather from him, he's being paid by someone," Cora shared.

"By whom?" Markway stood, fury evident on his face.

River swallowed hard, not ever wanting to be on his bad side.

"He didn't say, but he did allude to the war between wolves. I'm not sure what is going on, but I believe wolves are behind this."

Growls echoed in the room between Markway, the alpha, and the alpha's men who were out in the hallway. His gaze cut over to Evan.

"What is going on, Councilman?" Evan asked. He stood to his full height, folding his arms in front of him. "Is there something the council has not shared with the alphas? If there is war brewing, we should have been alerted to this immediately."

"There are those wanting a war. After talking to my granddaughter, I looked into a few things. What I am about to tell you needs to be spoken in private," Markway said.

Evan went over to the door and spoke quietly amongst his men, sending them away.

"Come, River. We can give them a moment." Cora motioned for her to follow.

"No, the two of you will need to hear this. Especially you, River," Markway said.

Evan shut the door and walked over to them.

"How sensitive is the information you are about to share?" Cora asked.

"Very. Would you mind?" Markway lifted an eyebrow to Cora.

"It would be an honor." Cora closed her eyes, and within seconds, River picked up the sound of a ward falling into place around them. Cora created a sealed environment where no one would be able to hear their conversation. She opened her eyes and winked at River.

Show-off, River mouthed to her.

"I thought I was protecting my granddaughter, but it would appear every decision I have made has put her in the line of danger," the councilman began.

River stiffened at his word choice.

"What do you mean?" Evan asked, obviously confused as well.

"The stripping of an alpha of his pack and

powers hasn't been done in centuries. When the esteemed council has to step in, it is always with the intention of keeping our people safe. Barone Westway had to be dealt with. By stripping him as alpha, we opened the door for pushback from supporters of his," Markway said.

River swallowed hard. She couldn't imagine what hard decisions he'd had to make in his position. She glanced at her mate lying still beside her. Kardia's chest rose and fell steadily.

"Alphas are not to go against the council. The council's word is law," Evan growled.

"Well, there are those who would like to challenge the ways we've existed for a long time, Evan. It's mostly younger alphas who are not educated properly on the good old days."

"Then it sounds as if they would need to be taught a lesson."

"And that is how they would get the way they are demanding. We've kept much of this quiet, trying to develop a fail-safe."

"How?"

"We have formed a secondary council should the one currently in place become corrupted."

"Second council—" Evan was cut off by Markway raising his hand.

"In the event that the heirs to the seat of the current one are compromised, the second council will have the power to overturn the primary members," Markway explained. "We have been thinking of everything that will secure the future of wolves everywhere."

"You don't trust your own heir?" Evan asked.

Markway shook his head vehemently. His gaze landed on Kardia. His facial features softened as he took in his granddaughter.

"I don't, and neither does Kardia," he replied softly.

"But your heir is your son, her father?" River said in disbelief. She knew the family dynamics between Kardia and her father were on a thin line, but this was madness.

"If I had my way, Kardia would be my heir." He turned his attention to River. He stepped closer to her, resting a hand on her shoulder. "Since she is not my heir, I have named her to my family's seat on the second council."

"What?" River gasped.

"Each council member had a choice in the seats, and there is no one I would trust more to go against her father than Kardia. She is a strong wolf who they have underestimated her entire life."

"You think her father is up to this?" River asked.

"I'm not one hundred percent sure. I pray my son hasn't crossed the line and would do something this extreme to his daughter."

"Then that would mean we would need to hurry and rescue Kardia," Cora said.

"And you think you can do this?" Markway asked.

"Cora is extremely powerful. I have the absolute faith she could," Evan said.

"We would need to act tonight. If you go to the Realm of Shadows, then I'm sure we can get it out of him. I wasn't at my full powers the last time I was there. Now if I physically go, he won't be able to stop me," Cora growled.

"Then I'm going with you," Markway said. By the hardness in his voice, River could tell he was not leaving any room for them to say no.

"River, are you going with them?" Evan asked.

"Of course. I can't sit by and do nothing," she said. She reached up and tucked her thick hair behind her ear. "If she is injured, then I can help with healing her."

Kardia didn't want to think that her mate was injured, but it was a great possibility. Cora had shared that she had tried to heal her. She'd reported that Kardia had been covered in wounds and suffering pain with them. She'd placed a temporary healing spell on her that would have covered her until they had left the realm and she could return to her real body. For all River knew, that spell could have been broken and Kardia would be just as Cora had found her.

"Then while you all are gone, we shall protect Kardia. You don't have to worry about her animal. She will be safe amongst us," Evan assured them. He turned to Markway. "Do you want some of my wolves to accompany you?"

"No, I have my own." Markway shook his head. "But thank you for the offer. I want you and your men on high alert here. There is no telling what will come to Howling Valley. We can't assume they won't come for her wolf."

"I agree." Evan nodded.

River trusted the alpha. He had welcomed her mate with open arms and he was a good alpha to his pack. Someone needed to ensure nothing happened to her body, so that once they rescued her mind, she could merge again with herself. River shivered, thinking that someone would come and try to take her mate's body.

"Then it's settled. Let's meet in one hour's time. Gather what you need. Beware, the Realm of Shadows is extremely dangerous," Cora warned. She gave the location of where they were to meet. It wasn't far from where they were.

Evan and Markway moved over to the door, deep in conversation.

River sat on the edge of the bed and ran a hand through Kardia's fur. She leaned over and pressed a kiss to her mate's head.

"I'm coming for you, my love. Hold on just a little longer," she whispered into Kardia's ear. She prayed Kardia heard her. She finally had Kardia's wolf here with her, but she needed the two of them together.

"Are you sure you're up to this?" Cora asked softly.

"What would you do if it were Addy's mind trapped in another realm?" River asked, not taking her eyes off her mate's wolf.

"I'd be readying myself to fight every magic wielder in the world for her."

"And that's what I'm going to do."

River met Cora's gaze. She may be a witch with healing powers, but she still knew how to defend herself. If going to the Realm of Shadows meant saving her mate, then she'd prepare for war.

River folded her arms in front of her to ward off the chill. She wasn't sure why the temperature around them was dropping so sharply. It had been nice earlier, and she didn't remember the weatherman calling for cold weather this week.

They were located deep in the woods near a cliff. The full moon was high. There were no clouds near it. The orb shined bright in the dark night, casting down its rays around them.

Cora stood next to her, muttering something in an ancient language. They had been waiting for Markway and his men to arrive. It wasn't long until the councilman appeared. He was dressed in casual clothing and had two big, scary-looking men with him.

"We are ready," he said, stopping in front of Cora and River.

"Welcome," Cora said, her eyes snapping open. She had dark leather clothing while River was in leggings and a loose t-shirt. She had a satchel filled with healing herbs and supplies she may need. She didn't know what she was going to find when they arrived at Kardia.

"This is Fitcher and Sheng. They are my personal guards who will provide protection for us," he said.

They exchanged pleasantries before all eyes turned to Cora.

"I will open a portal that will take us directly to the Realm of Shadows. I'm hoping I remembered the exact location of Kardia and where he was holding her. I'm praying he is too cocky and hasn't moved her. I'm assuming he thinks he has scared me off from returning." Cora smirked.

"Get us as close as you can and we can track her," Markway said.

"Stay close. It's not called the Realm of Shadows for nothing," Cora warned. She swiveled and took a few steps away. She raised her hands, chanting words in an ancient tongue.

River watched in awe how she was able to open the portal alone. A large, circular void with shimmering light was awaiting them.

Cora turned and waved them on. "After you."

Markway and his men stepped through first. River followed behind them with Cora coming after her. The portal sealed shut with a loud bang.

River stumbled from the force but was able to catch herself before falling. She spun around and took in the creepy surroundings.

She'd never been to another realm before. Now was not the time to explore. She was on a mission to rescue her mate.

The area around them was eerily dark and the air filled with magic.

"We are not that far." Cora walked to the front of their group.

They stood in the midst of a thick wooded area on the side of a mountain. There was a path that led into complete darkness. The hairs on the back of River's neck rose as she stared into the void.

"She's located up there." Cora pointed to an area that was higher up.

River swallowed hard but pushed down her fear. She could do this. Kardia was counting on them to help.

"You have nothing to fear," Markway said. He and his men surrounded her.

They must have scented her fear. She knew that wolves had very sensitive noses.

"Thank you. Once we get to Kardia, then I will feel much better." She exhaled and switched her attention to where Kardia was being kept.

Determination filled her. She would help her mate.

"We need to hurry and stay quiet. Dashiel may have eyes in the woods," Cora warned.

They began the trek up the mountain. River was tucked in between Fitcher and Sheng. She held on to the strap of her bag, walking with the two wolves. Markway strolled along with Cora. The four of them remained silent. River strained to listen around them, but she didn't hear anything in the woods.

"What's wrong?" Fitcher asked.

River jumped at his question. They had been walking in silence for a while, and it was the first time she'd heard his voice.

"Just nervous, worried, and afraid." Her voice shook.

Markway held a hand up for them to pause. If she didn't know any better, she would say the trees were closing in on them. She glanced behind him, and the path they had been walking was no longer. A gasp escaped her as she stared in the direction they had just come.

How was that possible?

Were the trees moving?

River took a step backward, bumping into Fitcher.

"Come closer," Cora whispered. She held her fingers up to her lips. She motioned toward the trees River had been staring at. "Everything is a living being here. The trees can move but should be harmless."

River's eyes widened.

Should be harmless?

She gulped and was thankful the two wolves stayed close to her. She quickly moved to stand next to Cora. It was then she could hear voices off in the distance.

"Who is that?" River asked, keeping her voice down.

They crept forward, stopping at the edge of the woods. She peered through the brush and took in a tall, cloaked figure standing in front of two men. In the dark, River couldn't make out many details of the men. One of them had long locs that went past his shoulders while the other one was bald. They were both large, muscular, and there was no mistaking them for anything other than wolves.

"Can you dispose of her?" The man with locs asked. He almost sounded bored, folding his arms in front of his chest.

"You didn't pay me for that. You wanted the girl, I brought her to you," the cloaked figure replied.

"We wanted a whole girl, not just her mind," the other man snapped. He motioned to the cave behind him. "What are we to do with just her mind? We aren't warlocks."

"The mind and body cannot survive without each other. Soon, you won't have to worry about what to do with her. Nature will take care of itself." The cloaked figure chuckled.

"Where is her body?" Locs asked.

"How would I know?" The cloaked figure shrugged.

They were talking about Kardia. But who were these men?

"The one in the cloak is Dashiel. He's the warlock who took Kardia. He's the one who put the curse on her all those years ago," Cora responded.

"And those two men who are with him are wolves," Markway snarled. His amber eyes glowed brightly.

Fitcher and Sheng released low growls.

"You recognize them?" Cora asked.

"I certainly do. The one with the locs is my grandson, Ruston, and the one with him is his friend, Hawes," Markway seethed. He turned toward Fitcher and Sheng. "I didn't want to believe my own flesh and blood would so something like this. You are to take them alive. They will answer for their crimes publicly."

River's heart lurched. Her mate's own brother was the one who'd had her cursed.

"What is the plan? We can't just walk out there and expect they will roll over and hand Kardia over to us," River asked. She was ready to go after her mate.

"Dashiel is mine," Cora announced. She jerked her head to Markway. "You take care of the wolves, and River, once the protective ward is down in front of the cave, you dash in there and check out your mate. Protect her. Do what you must. Whatever will happen to her here in this realm is real."

River shivered at Cora's words. Her friend didn't need to say more. If Kardia died here, her body back home would die.

"No one will touch my mate," River vowed. Kardia would be in the best of hands.

"Once everything is clear, I will come for you." Cora reached for her hand and gave it a squeeze.

"But how will you return her mind to her body?" Markway asked.

Cora smiled and glanced over at the wolf.

"That is the easy part once I break Dashiel's hold on her." Cora released River's hand and offered a smile. "Stay here until you hear my signal."

"What will that be?" River asked.

"Oh, you'll know."

CHAPTER SIXTEEN

Kardia heard voices outside her cave. She strained to hear them, and one of them was eerily familiar. If she wasn't mistaken, it sounded like her brother.

The bottom of her stomach sank as she came to the realization that it was Ruston's voice.

"Where is her body?" Ruston asked.

Tears blurred Kardia's vision. Even though she had suspected her family was out to get her, she had hoped and prayed that her suspicions were wrong. Her brother, someone she had grown up with, played with as a child, had chosen to eliminate her.

As they had gotten older, the changes in her

brother was obvious. Her father had always treated him differently. Ruston was their father's heir, making him the future of their family. His children would carry on their family name.

Was the seat on the secondary council worth her life?

Apparently, he thought so. Now she needed to know if her father was in on this scheme, too. Her heart was already broken by her brother's deceit. It would be shattered if her father was involved. She'd always hoped that deep down inside, they had loved her. It may not be the traditional love that most experienced, but she had hoped they loved her in their own way.

Kardia stood, bracing her arm to her side, and crept to the mouth of the cave so she could see Ruston with her own eyes. Kardia wished her grandfather was here to see her brother and his evil ways. She knew her grandfather hadn't wanted to hear her accusation, but she had felt that someone close to her was responsible for the curse.

Now she had her confirmation.

She peered out into the darkness and stood as tall as she could. She could easily make out her brother's figure. Next to him was his lackey of a friend, Howes. Rage filled her as she watched them speak about her as if she was not a living being.

Discard her? What was she, trash?

As long as she had breath in her body, she wouldn't give up her seat. If her grandfather believed she was the best person for the job, then it would be hers. She prepared herself, ready to fight. She may not have her wolf, and was weaken from her attack, but she would give her all.

"What was that?" Ruston shouted.

A loud howl came from the darkness. Kardia paused, recognizing the wolf's call. It had been a while since she'd heard the sound, but she would recognize it anywhere.

"It's not possible."

Her brother turned, their gazes clashing with one another. His amber eyes glowed in the dark. The hatred he had for her was visible even from where she stood. Greed and the need for power was consuming him. It didn't take much for her to see that.

"Once I'm done with the old man, I'll be back for you, dear sister." He pointed to her before he and Howes raced off out of her sight.

"Is that truly you, Papa?" she wondered aloud.

Was that her grandfather? And if it was, how was he here in this realm?

Cora.

Had the witch returned with reinforcements?

"That witch apparently didn't learn her lesson." Dashiel turned his attention on Kardia. He took a menacing step toward her.

Kardia took a step back away from the mouth of the cave. A dark cloud of energy lifted from the ground and surrounded him.

"I see I'm going to have to teach her who rules the Realm of Shadows. She has no power—" His body flew forward, a white bolt of energy slamming into his side, cutting his words off.

Kardia's heart leaped with hope. She was being rescued. She didn't know how, but the witch had returned and brought reinforcements with her.

Dashiel pushed off the ground with a shout. The hood fell off of his head, revealing long, dark hair. He waved his hand, and large chunks of the earth lifted and flew toward his attacker. He charged forward, disappearing into the night.

The sounds of fighting echoed through the air. Kardia wished she was free to see her grandfather take her brother down. Ruston always was cocky and hotheaded, but he would be no match for her grandfather who was older and experienced. Knowing her grandfather, he would have his best men with him. Ruston and Howes would be fools to fight the councilmen's guards. They were deadly wolves. Her brother wasn't a warrior who had fought in battles like the guards.

Kardia grew weak standing. Her breaths were becoming labored. She moved to the wall closest to the entrance and leaned against it. She slid down and sat down before her legs gave out.

"What is wrong with me?' she whispered. What energy she had was fading.

"*The mind and body cannot survive without each other. Soon, you won't have to worry about what to do with her. Nature will take care of itself.*" Dashiel's words echoed through her head. Was her mind beginning to shut down? Panic blossomed in her chest. She wasn't ready to die. She had to see River one last time.

She leaned her head back against the rocky wall and sent up a prayer to the gods. She prayed to all of them, hoping one would hear her plea.

Let me see my mate one last time. Allow me to tell her I love her, and then you can take me.

Her weakness was growing. Her limbs were heavy. Her eyelids were barely able to blink.

Fate was cruel. Not only had she allowed

Kardia to find her mate, she would proceed to take the woman away, and then allow an evil warlock to separate her from her animal. She had always thought she would die as a wolf. Tears spilled from her eyes, falling down her face. How had her life become so broken? What had she done to deserve this?

The sound of glass shattering filled the air, but Kardia didn't have the strength to respond. What around her was made of glass? Kardia didn't think anything was. She remembered the cold, hard rock of the cave she'd been trapped in. Her shoulders slumped, more of her energy dissipating.

"Kardia!"

Warm hands gripped her shoulder. She grimaced from the pain that exploded. Her head rolled forward. She was too weak to lift it.

"Can you hear me? Kardia?" The voice was familiar.

Kardia blinked, trying to remember where she knew the voice from. Her mouth moved, but no words escaped her. Soft fingers gently raised her chin and tilted her head back. She opened her eyes and stared into a familiar set of eyes. It took her a moment before recognition broke through.

River.

Her mate.

Surely she was hallucinating. Was this how she would go out? Hallucinate and see her mate before she drifted into oblivion?

"River?" she whispered.

"Yes, it's me. Oh my. What have they done to you?" River hiccuped. Her mate released her and reached for a satchel that was on the ground next to them. "I'm going to fix you all up, and then we are going to get you home."

"I don't have time," Kardia said. Her voice was weak, and she wished she had more power to project herself louder.

"What?" River turned back to her while crushing some herbs together in a small bowl. She poured a liquid in it, turning back to Kardia. "Here, I need you to eat this."

Kardia pushed her hand away from her face. She needed to tell River how she felt. She may not ever get another chance. She had prayed to the gods, and one of them must have heard her. It was the only reason River was here. Now she had to keep her bargain.

"River—"

"Please, eat this." River tried to force-feed her what was on the spoon.

"I have to tell you something first. I—" Kardia's sight was failing. The dark cave was growing even darker. What little light that flowed in from the moon was disappearing. She could barely make River out.

"What is it, my love?"

"I love you, River. I love you with everything I have," Kardia breathed. She reached out and felt for River. She ignored the pain. Her hands landed on River's arms. She inhaled, breathing in her mate's scent. She would never forget this. She smiled, content that she was able to tell River her true feelings for her.

"Oh, I love you, too. Now I need you to eat this."

Kardia allowed her to stuff her mouth with the spoon. The concoction on it was absolutely horrible. She coughed a few times, finally swallowing it. She didn't know what it was, but she was sure her mate thought she would be able to save her.

"You love me, too?" Kardia asked, her voice barely audible.

"Of course I do, silly." River's warm lips pressed to Kardia's forehead. Her hands came to settle on Kardia's cheeks. "You have to stay with me. No going to sleep."

"But I'm so tired. So weak. I can't. I'm sorry."

"Kardia. Open your eyes. Stay with me," River pleaded. She shook Kardia by the shoulders. "You have to hold on. Cora is here. She's going to send you back to your body."

"My wolf..." Kardia didn't have any energy to speak. It pained her to think that her wolf was gone.

"Your wolf is back home. The alpha, Evan, is watching over her. I left her to come find you."

Kardia opened her eyes at the news. Her wolf was safe. Finally, her wolf was free. A smile came to her lips. Could Cora save the two of them? If Kardia didn't reconnect with her wolf soon, she would fade, and if that happened, then her wolf would die as well.

"That's it." River smiled. "Stay with me."

A warmth settled in Kardia's chest. She didn't know what her mate had made her eat, but something was happening. A burst of energy rippled from her core and radiated throughout her body. River took advantage of her stillness to explore her wounds. She talked gently while she worked on making a salve and putting it on her deepest wound on her shoulder.

Kardia listened quietly as River shared with her

the trip to this realm. She confirmed that indeed, Wyett was with them. Kardia knew she would always be able to count on her grandfather. He would never let her down.

"Now, you should feel a little better." River settled back on her haunches and stared at Kardia. She took her hands in hers and kissed the back of them. "The moment you are home and have your strength, I am binding myself to you. We are claiming each other. No matter if we are whole or not. I would rather have half of you than none of you."

Tears appeared in Kardia's eyes. She smiled softly and nodded. She couldn't agree more. If she made it out of here, she would claim her mate. Waiting had been a mistake.

"Where is my granddaughter?" Wyett's voice filled the cave.

Kardia turned slightly and took in her grandfather striding toward her. He was naked, fresh from a shift. His long locs flowed down his back. He came to kneel on the other side of her. He took her hand in his.

"It's all over for now, Kardia. Your brother will pay for everything."

"Are you okay?" she asked.

"You are literally fading before my eyes and you are worried about me." Wyett chuckled. He leaned forward and kissed her forehead. "I would run through fire to save you. Of course I am fine. Did you think your brother would be a match for me?"

She shook her head. The little burst of energy that was in the concoction River had given her was starting to leave her. She felt herself slowing weakening again.

"Is the fighting over?" River asked.

"Yes, Cora should be here in a moment. My men are with my grandson and his friend." Wyett gave Kardia the once-over. A growl escaped him at the sight of all of her wounds. "What can I do for you?"

"You've already done so much for me," she whispered. There was a tortured expression she'd never seen on his face before. She squeezed his hand. "I love you, Papa."

"You tell me that when we get home and you are whole with your wolf." He patted her on the back of her hand.

Footsteps sounded behind them. They all turned and took in Cora entering the cave. The witch was dressed in a black leather outfit. She looked like a total badass witch, and Kardia was glad she was on their side. She didn't know if she could handle being against two deranged witches.

"How is she?" Cora asked.

"Still with us," Wyett replied. He stood to give Cora room to come and kneel by her.

"You came back," Kardia murmured.

"I did. I told you I would get you home." Cora smiled at her. She took both of Kardia's hands in hers.

"I will see you soon." River leaned forward and kissed her cheek.

Kardia's gaze flew to River's before turning to Cora.

"What is about to happen?" Kardia asked.

"I am sending you back to where you belong," Cora said.

"Will it hurt?" Kardia asked. She'd been through enough pain recently. She just needed to brace herself if she had to go through more.

"Not at all. Do you trust me?" Cora asked. Her hands were growing warmer, and it was soothing to Kardia.

"Yes," she replied without hesitation.

"Close your eyes and inhale," Cora instructed.

Kardia did as she'd been told. Her eyes fluttered shut, and she breathed in deeply. Cora's two fingers pressed on the center of her forehead. A language Kardia had never heard of flowed from Cora. A burst of heat surged from her and flowed into Kardia.

Her body became weightless. She tried to open her eyes, but all she saw was darkness. No longer could she sense Cora or River near her. The sounds of the cave disappeared. A wave of energy traveled its way from the top of her head down to her toes.

Kardia's body flailed, and she felt herself falling through the air. Suddenly, she came to a halt. The breath in her lungs escaped. She jerked awake, her eyes flying open.

No longer was she in the cave. She blinked and looked around, finding herself in what appeared to be a hospital room with glass windows surrounding the room she was in. The scent of antiseptic was overly strong.

Where was she?

She lifted her head and gasped.

Raising her arm, she took in a paw covered in white fur. She glanced down at herself in disbelief.

She was in her wolf form.

"Welcome back to the land of the living."

She turned to the voice and took in the alpha

standing in the doorway watching her. Immediately, her wolf bowed her head to him.

Yes, it was good to be back in the land of the living and in her wolf form. Now all she needed was for her mate to come to her.

CHAPTER SEVENTEEN

"What did you do with Dashiel?" River asked, following Cora through the portal.

The councilman and his men walked ahead of them with their prisoners. When it came time for them to leave the Realm of Shadows, River had noticed the warlock was missing.

"Let's just say I sent him to another realm," Cora replied. She turned and waved her hand, shutting the entrance to the other realm.

River was glad to have left the spooky land. She was happy to be back on Earth.

"He wanted to practice dark magic, so I

magicked him somewhere he would be welcomed," Cora said.

River shivered. She didn't want to know where Cora had sent him. The witch had a cynical grin on her lips.

"Don't worry. I banished him to the land of enchantment. That realm is full of love and rainbows. It would be torture for him, and he can't do them any harm. Their queen owes me a favor. He won't be leaving there for a long time." Cora laughed.

River stared at her friend with wide eyes. She almost felt as if she didn't know her. Here she was, thinking Cora had forced him somewhere to be tortured, and in the end, she'd put him in some magical realm that would keep him from practicing dark magic?

"You never cease to amaze me." River shook her head. A reddish wolf appeared at the edge of the woods near them. "Looks like someone decided to meet you."

"Yeah, I'm sure she was missing me."

River waved to Addy in her wolf form. The wolf flicked her head in acknowledgement. A wolfy grin appeared on her lips.

"Do you need me for anything else?" Cora asked.

"No, you've done so much. I don't know how we can thank you," River admitted.

"Go to your mate and make sure she's okay. If you need me, I'm just a phone call away." Cora took a step back away from her and gave a wave.

"Go to Addy." River motioned for her to go. She turned and headed in the direction of the councilman.

His men loaded his grandson and friend up in the back of a van and slammed the door shut.

"I can give you a ride since I'm sure we are going to the same place," Markway said.

"I'd appreciate it."

River walked alongside the councilman over to the car that was parked behind the van. Markway and his men grabbed clothes from the trunk and put them on. She knew shifters were not shy about being nude. She'd been around enough of them to know that being naked was second nature to them. She waited by the car while they dressed.

River couldn't stop thinking of Kardia. Had she woken up yet? Was she whole? It didn't matter to River. If she couldn't shift, that wasn't going to keep her from binding herself to her wolf.

Fitcher opened the back door for her and helped her in the car. Soon they were on their way. It didn't take long before they were arriving at the Nightstar Pack infirmary. River and Markway headed toward the front of the building but were met by the pack's beta, Mick, coming out of the door. The two men shook hands in greeting.

"River. It's been a long time since I've seen you," Mick said, turning to her.

"Likewise. How's the family?" she asked.

"Everyone is doing well." He laughed. "But I'm sure you both are here to see Kardia. She's out back with Evan. Head around the building and follow the walkway that will lead you to the back. You'll see them."

River didn't have to be told twice. She took off almost at a sprint and raced around the building. Dawn was approaching. The sky was becoming a mixture of orange and yellows. She couldn't wait for the morning where she and Kardia could sit out in the yard and watch the sunrise together. She made it to the back of the building and scanned the area. The infirmary was located near the pack's lodge that was deep in the forest. She didn't see any signs of her mate.

"Kardia!" she called out. She was too excited to

wait for her. She felt Markway come up behind her. A howl off in the distance sent a ripple of anticipation through her body.

"She heard you," Markway said.

"That was her?" River practically jumped in place. She could hardly stay still. She was anxious to run off in the woods to find Kardia.

"It was. She's on her way." He chuckled.

River took a few steps forward and caught sight of a dash of white. She squinted, trying to see through the woods. Finally, two wolves came streaking out of the trees. One black and one white. The black one was twice the size of the white one. Evan must be the black one. Her gaze landed on the white wolf, and River immediately took off running toward her.

Kardia's wolf grinned as she made her way to her. Once they were close enough, she leaped into the air and crashed into River. She laughed, falling to the ground with her wolf on top of her. Finally, they were able to meet. River rolled around with her wolf, but Kardia was tricky and landed back on top of River. The wolf bathed River's face with her tongue. River laughed, basking in the joy of having her mate in her wolf form. Kardia had waited so long to be able to shift and run free as her animal.

"You're such a beauty," River said, running her fingers through Kardia's thick fur.

Kardia's animal bent her head down and licked River's face again. River wrapped her arms around the beast and hugged her tight. She released Kardia and rested her hands on the wolf's face.

"I need to speak with Kardia."

The wolf whined, nuzzling her face into the crook of River's neck. River laughed, sensing the wolf didn't want to go back.

"Now that you are free, you can come out anytime, but I really need to talk with Kardia. Please?" she asked softly.

Kardia whined. She gave River one last lick before lifting her head. She caught sight of her grandfather and yipped at him.

"I see you, Kardia," Markway said. He stood next to the alpha who had already shifted back to his human form.

Kardia stepped away from River. She gave her another wolfish grin, the air around her shimmering. River watched in awe as her lover transitioned from her beautiful white wolf to her beautiful, brown-skinned woman. Kardia knelt on the ground, naked as the day she was born. She raised her head and met River's gaze. They stood, not breaking their gaze. They stepped toward each other until they were close.

"You are fully healed?" River whispered. Her gaze roamed Kardia's body, and she didn't see any of the marks that had marred her body while in the Realm of the Shadows.

"I am." Kardia's eyes filled with tears that spilled down her cheeks. She reached for River and pulled her into a tight hug.

River wrapped her arms around the love of her life, unable to keep her tears from falling.

"Thank you."

"You don't have to thank me for anything." River sniffed. She tightened her hold on Kardia, not ever wanting to let her go. She officially had her mate in her arms and she wanted her to stay there forever. "You belong to me, and they had no right to take you from me."

"Where is he?" Kardia asked.

"Ruston and Howes will pay for their crimes," Markway announced. He must have overheard Kardia's question. "The alpha has agreed to lock them up in their jail until they can be transferred to the council's prison to await their trials. We will be investigating who else is involved and get to the bottom of this."

"The Nightstar Pack will assist in any way we can," Evan said. "Just let us know what we can do, and we will help.

"It's officially over?" Kardia whispered.

"It is." Markway came to stand in front of them. He smiled and reached out a hand to rest it on Kardia's shoulder. "Go home, claim your mate, and get some rest. All in that order. If we need you, we'll call you."

"Can I speak—"

"No," Markway interjected without hearing what Kardia was going to ask. "You don't need to speak with your brother. I will handle him. You and I will have a long talk later, but for now, go home."

Kardia nodded and turned to River. Love shined bright in her eyes. River agreed with Markway. Kardia shouldn't try to speak with her brother. He'd had her cursed and tried to kill her. That trauma would live with Kardia for a while. Now was the time she needed to start healing and to move forward with her life. That was where River came in.

Kardia leaned her forehead on River's while a smile played on her lips.

"Your place or mine?" River asked.

"Whoever's place is the closest."

K ardia stared at her slumbering mate. River lay naked underneath the blanket with her newly claimed mark on her shoulder. Kardia felt immense pride that her mate finally wore her mark. Her witch had bonded to her. She felt the link between them in her heart and she couldn't be any happier.

It wasn't too long ago that she thought she was going to be dying and the only wish she had was to be able to see River one last time and tell her she loved her. Kardia was grateful that she'd got a second chance at life. One thing she'd learned was that she never wanted to be separated from her wolf or mate again.

Kardia slipped from the bed and walked over to the window of her cabin. Her place had been closest. The moment they'd stepped foot inside, they'd both had one thing on their minds.

Sealing the bond between the two of them.

Kardia stared at the dark sky. They had spent all day in bed, and now it was nighttime again. She wouldn't complain. After their marathon love-making and claiming, they had slept most of the day.

Kardia exhaled softly, watching the stars that littered the dark sky. She smiled, thankful for everything she had. Her wolf was content. Not only had she been able to race through the woods with the alpha, she'd been able to sink her fangs into River's flesh and claim her.

Her wolf had no complaints at the moment.

Kardia's ears picked up the sound of River moving in the bed.

"What are you doing up?" River's soft voice came from behind her. Footsteps padded toward her. River's warm body pressed against her back as she wrapped her arms around Kardia's waist.

"I'm fully rested and wanted to look outside. I didn't wake you, did I?" Kardia asked. She turned around in River's arms and took in her beautiful mate. She reached up and cupped River's cheeks. Kardia was in awe that this woman was officially hers for all eternity.

"Not having you by my side woke me up." River smiled.

"Is that so?" Kardia kissed River's lips softly.

Her mate's mouth immediately opened, granting her tongue entrance. Their kiss was slow and deep with them pressing close to each other. Their naked breasts slid along each other, sending a ripple of desire through Kardia. Even though she'd had her mate countless times today, she still wanted her.

It would always be this way between the two of them.

Kardia broke the kiss and blazed a trail of kisses along River's jawline and down to her neck. When she came to her claiming mark, she licked it a few times to ensure it would heal properly. The enzymes in her tongue would help it along. She'd be left with a beautiful mark that would declare she was mated to Kardia. The scent of her mate's arousal drifted in the air. She inhaled, breathing in the sweet, tangy scent.

"Come back to bed, my love," River whispered.

Her hand skated down Kardia's torso and slipped between them. Her fingers parted Kardia's folds and arrived at her swollen clit. Kardia gasped, leaning into River's hand. Her mate walked backward, guiding Kardia to the bed. She spun them around until Kardia landed on the mattress. River crawled on and lay beside her with her hand still between Kardia's thighs. Her fingers stroked Kardia's swollen nub before slipping into her warm channel.

Kardia moaned, spreading her legs wider to allow River to push her fingers deeper.

"You know just what to do to get me to do what you want." Kardia chuckled.

River leaned down and captured her nipple in her mouth. She reached up and gripped the sheets in her hands, turning her pleasure over to her mate.

"Of course I do," River admitted. She trailed her tongue around Kardia's breast while thrusting a second finger inside her. "You see you are now back in the bed, right?"

Kardia barked a laugh that soon died as she watched River slide down the bed and position herself where her face was level with her pussy. River withdrew her fingers and licked them clean. She pressed her hands on the back of Kardia's legs, holding them open.

"I love you, River," Kardia whispered. She vowed that she would always make sure she knew how much she loved her.

"I love you, too."

River took a long lick of her slit that sent Kardia's body arching off the bed. Kardia gripped the sheets tighter. She heard them tear slightly but ignored it. She would worry about purchasing a new set later. "Now that I know what will get you to do as I say, tomorrow, I will start taming that wolf of yours."

River's tongue dipped down into her heat before sliding back to her clit. River's fingers parted Kardia's folds, exposing her sensitive clitoris. She wrapped her lips around it, suckling it into her mouth so hard it snatched a cry from Kardia. One of her hands released the sheet and immediately flew to River's head. She threaded her fingers into her mate's thick hair to hold her in place.

"Taming her? Don't you know you've already got her wrapped around your pinkie?" Kardia gasped. There wasn't anything her wolf wouldn't do for River.

"Good. Now lie back and let me pleasure you."

Kardia didn't have to be told twice.

EPILOGUE

The past two months had flown by. Kardia and River had decided to move into River's home. It was larger and would allow them to expand should they decide to start a family. River couldn't remember ever being so happy.

Kardia had finally settled into Howling Valley. She had accepted a position at the local florist shop. She loved it, and River couldn't be happier for her.

River reached for a few glasses out of the cupboard, moving to the fridge. She grabbed a pitcher filled with freshly squeezed lemonade she'd made yesterday evening. She poured three glasses and placed them on a tray along with the pitcher, then headed outside.

Kardia and Markway sat in the rocking chairs on the porch, deep in conversation. From the moment Markway had called and announced he was coming for a visit, Kardia had been a nervous wreck.

He had refused to allow her to be involved with her brother's trial. Kardia was frustrated with it, but River agreed with the councilman. Her mate had been through so much. River trusted that he would take care of it as he'd promised.

"Here she is," Markway said. He was dressed in his long, regal robes today and looked like a king.

She walked over and held the tray out for him to take his glass. She moved over to Kardia next who took hers. River set the tray down on the table before them and picked up her glass. She settled in the rocker next to Kardia.

"I'm back. What did I miss?" she asked.

"I was just sharing the good news with Kardia. Ruston was sentenced by the council. He has been given twenty years in Purgatory for his crimes and has been stripped of all claims to the council. When he is released, he will not be able to pursue any office or seat."

"Twenty years is a long time to think of what he's done and grow even more angry with me," Kardia said. She lifted her glass to her lips and sipped.

"Coming after a councilwoman would be dangerous for his health," Markway growled.

"So, my father?"

"From what I can tell, he had no part of Ruston's scheme to take you out. Your father was interrogated by the council and investigated. As you know, our investigations are very thorough. There is nothing that could be hidden from the council."

Kardia grew silent.

"What is it?" River reached out and took Kardia's hand.

"I feel horrible. I had thought my father had a part in my curse and everything. I just assumed—"

"Now, your father hasn't been a saint. He's done you wrong over the years, and we have had a long conversation about how he and your mother have treated you."

"What?" Kardia gasped.

Markway turned to her, setting his glass down on the table.

"This conversation your father and I had was long overdue. He had better clean up his act. If he doesn't, I will revoke his claim as my heir, and he knows it. As of now, you will still be a member of the second council. They will be reaching out to you soon for a meeting."

"I understand." Kardia smiled. She squeezed River's hand and sat forward. "I'd be willing to sit down and talk with them. It's past time for us to have a family meeting."

River knew that it had taken a lot for Kardia to say that. Part of her healing would be forgiveness. River would be right at Kardia's side through it all. This was her mate, and she would help her.

"Well, I don't want to tie up too much of you girls day. I have a meeting with Evan that I need to get to."

They moved to stand with him, but he waved them down.

"No need to get up. I can see myself around the house. My guards are out front waiting for me."

He moved over and pressed a kiss to each of their foreheads. Since their mating, he had treated River as a granddaughter. He gave a wave and disappeared around the house, leaving them alone.

"Are you okay?" River asked.

"I am. I know that eventually I need to forgive them. We don't have to have a close relationship, but we need to clear the air and put everything on the table."

"And I'll be right there with you." River squeezed her hand.

She smiled as Kardia tugged her onto her lap. River wrapped her arms around Kardia's neck. She leaned her head down and kissed her wolf. Kardia reached up and cupped her cheek while their kiss deepened. She tilted her head to the side, sending her tongue inside Kardia's mouth. She stroked Kardia's, lost in the kiss.

River pulled back from her, breaking the kiss.

"What do you want to do today?" Kardia asked.

"Let's go for a run," River suggested. She stood from Kardia's lap and backed up. She went down the few steps that put her down on the grass.

"Are you sure?"

"I can outrun you," River teased. She untied her dress straps that were secured at the base of her neck. Her dress slid down to the ground. She quickly got rid of her strapless bra and panties, leaving her naked. She walked backward, show-casing her body.

"You think you can?" Kardia pulled her t-shirt over her head and got rid of her shorts. Their clothes were now in two piles on the ground. "I'll even give you a head start."

Kardia fell to the grass, giving in to her animal. River turned around and took off running across the yard. She pumped her arms hard, running down the soft dirt path that led into the woods behind their home. She laughed, hearing her mate howl behind her. It wouldn't take long for Kardia to catch up to her.

There was something about the thrill of being chased.

River broke through the clearing just as a force slammed into her. She fell into the soft grass, and her white wolf lay on top of her. River's giggles filled the air. No matter how many times she'd teased and challenged her mate, Kardia fell for it every time.

Kardia threw back her head and let out another howl. Off in the distance, a few other wolves replied. Kardia's amber eyes locked on her. The air around them shimmered. Kardia shifted back into her human form. Her soft body molded to River's.

"You will never outrun me," Kardia murmured.

She leaned down and nipped River's bottom lip. Her fangs peeked through with her smile. River wrapped her arms around Kardia's neck and brought her face down to hers. They shared soft kisses before Kardia nuzzled River's neck. She gently bit River over her claiming bite again. It sent a bolt of electricity down to her core. She gasped, opening her legs to allow Kardia to settle in the valley of her thighs.

"I will try just to keep you and your wolf on your toes." River gasped. She tilted her head to the side to allow her mate to have her way with her.

Kardia's tongue slid along her wound, sealing it.

River's body trembled from the anticipation of what was to come.

"Well then, I will come for you every single time."

Kardia covered her mouth with hers in a deep, passionate kiss.

River wouldn't have it any other way.

Want to stay updated on Ariel Marie's releases, sign up for her mailing list!

LETTER FROM THE AUTHOR

Dear Reader,

We made it to book six. I never thought I would be writing so many books in this world. I'm so thankful for all of the readers who love visiting Howling Valley!

I hope you enjoyed meeting River and Kardia. This couple was so fun to write about. They and all the other couples have a special place in my heart.

Will I continue writing in this world? I'm not sure. I'm going to take a break and work on a few other sapphic paranormal stories I have in mind.

We'll see if any other characters from Howling Valley presents themselves to me.

Until then, I hope you enjoy my future books that are in the works!

Love,

Ariel Marie

Deadly Kiss

THE IMMORTAL REIGN 1

A vampire princess. A human. One drop of blood changed their lives forever.

Vampires had taken everything from Quinn Hogan during the war. She had spent her entire life hiding from them. The last thing Quinn wanted in life was to be matched to one. Each human was required by law to enter the draft. Her name was randomly picked for submitting her blood sample.

Chances of being chosen? A million to one.

Luck had never been on her side.

Quinn matched with a vampire.

Now she was being shipped off to some random vampire who would probably bleed her dry.

Velika Riskel didn't want a mate. As the warden

of Northwest America, there was no time for her to take a mate. When the human arrived, she had planned to release her, but one look into Quinn's hazel eyes and all of that changed.

Velika and Quinn's relationship was doomed from the start. Velika was a seasoned warrior who wasn't afraid of challenges. The vampire princess was determined to win Quinn's heart, defend her against a rival, and then claim her.

Don't miss this sexy, FF vampire romance tale.
Grab your copy today!

Moon Valley Shifters

A FF WOLF SHIFTER BOXSET

Three steamy stories of female shifters finding the mate destined for them. If you love sexy as sin, F/F wolf shifters paranormal romance stories, that will leave you breathless, then grab this hot box set!

Book 1 Lyric's Mate

Lyric moved to Moon Valley for a fresh start. A new town, a new home, and a new job was a dream come true. Finding that her new boss was her mate was totally unexpected. Will she be able to keep her wolf at bay?

Book 2 Meadow's Mate

Meadow, the new teacher in town had her eyes on the only female enforcer in the pack. Little did she know, the enforcer had Meadow in her sights. When a group of rogue wolves blows into town, will Sage be able to save her?

Book 3 Tuesday's Mate

Tuesday, the new accountant in town was setting up her new business in Moon Valley. Tuesday is entranced by Sunni, the coffee shop owner. Their wolves know they are meant for each other. But will Sunni and Tuesday listen to their beasts?

WARNING: These stories are sexy, fast-paced and will leave you begging for more.

Want to hear more from this tantalizing book?
Grab it t today!

The Dragon and Her Thief

A possessive dragon. A sexy thief. A job gone wrong...or did it?

Kelsey Rose wasn't crazy. She was determined. A family heirloom was stolen years ago, and she was the perfect person to recover it. No job was too big for her, but this one was going to be a challenge for her.

The only obstacle?

A dragon shifter.

Mythia Zinfina spent centuries protecting and growing her hoard. The powerful dragon shifter was patiently waiting for the day she would find her mate. Never did she expect the tiny slip of a woman breaking into her castle to be the one who was destined to be at her side for all eternity.

The second their eyes met, Mythia's dragon determined she would never let Kelsey go.

If you love steamy, wlw paranormal romance tales with plenty of heat and action, then you will enjoy The Dragon and Her Thief. This story was intended for mature readers only.

Don't miss this sexy, FF dragon shifter romance tale. Grab your copy today!

ABOUT THE AUTHOR

Ariel Marie is an author who loves the paranormal, action and hot steamy romance. She combines all three in each and every one of her stories. For as long as she can remember, she has loved vampires, shifters and every creature you can think of. This even rolls over into her favorite movies. She loves a good action packed thriller! Throw a touch of the supernatural world in it and she's hooked!

She grew up in Cleveland, Ohio where she currently resides with her husband and three beautiful children.

For more information:
www.thearielmarie.com

Also by Ariel Marie

Tiger Haven

Searching For His Mate

A Tiger's Gift

Stone Heart (The Gargoyle Protectors)

Saving Penny

A Beary Christmas

Howl for Me

Birthright

Return to Darkness

Red and the Alpha

The Dragon and Her Thief